The Ultimate Betrayal: A 336 Love Story

By:

I0632719

Erica Nicole

I dedicate this book my late grandfathers, Alfred "Sonnyboy" Barrett and William "Big Boy" Best. I love and miss you more than you'll ever know. Continue to rest in peace.

Acknowledgments: Thank you to my family and friends for supporting and encouraging me through this journey. A special thank you to my parents for praying me through the process. I love you all.

" This is my moment I've waited all my life I can that it's time"
- Nicki Minaj

Erica Best
Visit my website at www.enbestpublications.com

Printed in the United States of America

ISBN-13 978-1-7326969-1-4

Synopsis

Cherish Wright is a hopeless romantic who lives by the motto of love and loyalty until her relationship with Dame who was her college sweetheart goes sour. She's tired of mending a broken heart and determined to put the past behind her when she moves to the 336. A new city means a new attitude, except Cherish infatuation with love continues to be a blessing and a curse. On a quest to embrace the single life she meets Aaron, a young successful CEO of a major trucking company.

Aaron is a captivating businessman that operates like a tyrant. His self-entitled demeanor leaves an imprint on his love life as a lady's man who can get any woman he chooses until he meets Cherish. She's the type of woman that every guy dream of having and every female envy. She's a tough cookie, who's not fazed by his money, but Aaron savvy ways entices Cherish to let her guard down, opening the golden gate to her heart. Aaron presents himself as Mr. Perfect, but everything is not what it seems. Does he have what it takes to heal a broken heart and love her correctly?

For the past five years Kenly and Brittish have been Cherish's best friends. Kenly is deeply involved in a situationship. As much as Kenly wants loves, love doesn't seem to want her. For the sake of love Kenly's loving without limits, even if it means hurting someone in her inner circle. Then there's Brittish, the drama free and supportive friend that balances out the crew. She in a satisfying relationship with Grant, where everyone labels them as the "it" couple, until her lover intentions are questionable.

In this circle of friendship and love, remaining loyal is everything. Friendships are put to the test and love is on the line when the ultimate betrayal happens. Where does everybody's loyalty lies? Who's going to be disloyal to who in this love story?

Prologue

"Aye beautiful, would it hurt you to smile while you're working?"
I lifted my head from the register and looked around the student union
to figure out who he was talking to.

"You're looking around the union like you're confused or
something."

"I am confused. Who are you talking to?"

He stared at me with those eyes that were to die for. "Obviously,
you're not used to compliments. I was talking to you." I could tell by
the look in his eyes he was being sincere.

I started blushing, I'm surprised a man of his physique thinks I'm
beautiful. I know you're thinking I have low self-esteem, but that's not
the case. I'm just not used to being called beautiful while I'm in my
work uniform. Nothing about my collared yellow shirt with JCSU
student union embedded in the top right corner, khaki pants, and black
Vans was an appealing look, yet I was being complimented by one of
the finest men at John C. Smith University.

"Thanks. I don't hear too often that I'm beautiful while I'm
working."

"Well, just know you're beautiful as hell and never let no one tell
you anything different."

I started blushing again. "There goes that beautiful smile that was
hiding behind your mean mug expression." He reached out to touch
my cheek.

I couldn't help but burst out laughing. "I wasn't mean mugging
you. I'm just tired, and it's hard to smile when you've been on your
feet for seven hours."

"True that. Well, still try to smile anyways, you look more beautiful with that expression, versus that other look that you were rocking minutes ago." He reached into his wallet to pull out his golden bull's union card.

"If you don't mind me asking, I would love to take you out some time, whenever you're not working and don't have class."

I finished ringing him up and wrote my number down on the back of his receipt paper. "Bet, I'll text you, ma. Also, your name is Cherish, right?" he asked after looking down to read my name tag.

"Yes, you're correct." He wasn't shocked I already knew his name, as everybody who was remotely somebody on campus knew him. He grabbed his food and winked at me before walking out of the union.

I couldn't believe my country bama ass was going on a date with Dame. I'm originally from Memphis, Tennessee, and I came to North Carolina to go to college. I was ready for a change in scenery, and Charlotte was a dope city at the time.

I live up to the country bama standards of being cornbread and collard greens thick, with D cup breasts that sat up perfectly, and nah, my waist wasn't as slim as I would like for it to be, but it measured out with my apple shaped ass. I was dark chocolate with the same color eyes. I had a visible dimple on the right side of my face and a nose piercing. Many people often told me I resembled Tasha from the hit TV show Power.

I always wore my natural hair straight with a feathered side bang. Growing up in Memphis, I had always been told how gorgeous I was. I didn't let it get to my head though, I was raised to be humble.

A few days later, Dame and I finally had some downtime to go out on a date. It was six-fifteen p.m. when I applied my heroine MAC lipstick, and my phone started ringing.

"Hey beautiful, I'm downstairs in the common area. Are you ready yet?"

"I'm almost finishing with my makeup, then I'll be down."

"Bet ma, don't have me waiting on you too long."

I finished filling in my eyebrows, tossed my crossbody bag over my shoulder, and made my way downstairs. I could tell by Dame's eyes that he was feeling my fit. I loved the way his eyes could instantly tell what he was thinking. I wore a long-sleeved white t-shirt dress and a blush pair of heels from Fashion Nova.

"You look beautiful, as always, Cherish," he said, reaching out to give me a bear hug.

I caught myself blushing again as I said, "You look pretty handsome yourself."

We walked out the side door of my resident hall and hopped in Dame's 2014 black Camaro. We made small talk during our ride, but I couldn't help but feel nervous when I was in his presence. I had no clue where he was taking me, and I hoped I wasn't too overdressed for the night.

My favorite song titled "Primetime" by Janelle Monae ft. Miguel played on 102.1 jamz. I bobbed my head to the beat, but I couldn't refrain myself from singing along. "It's a prime time for our love, and heaven is betting on us..."

I was so into the song I didn't realize I had sung along to the very end. "You can carry a tune, and you're not afraid to be yourself, that's attractive," he stated, making me expose my dimple as I blushed.

"Thanks, I love to sing, even though I'm nowhere near Mariah Carey's level," I responded playfully, letting out a cute giggle. "But seriously though, that's my all-time favorite song. It speaks to my soul for the kind of love I want to have someday." Being open, honest, and basically being myself around him came naturally.

He kept one hand on the steering wheel, touching my soft hands with his free hand. "In the words of Janelle, "Maybe heaven is betting on us". I know it's too early to make assumptions, but I have a good feeling about you." I smiled inwardly knowing tonight was going to be one for the books.

Dame had taken me to a restaurant that's located in downtown Charlotte called 7th district. I immediately fell in love with this place as the lighting was dim and they played R&B music softly throughout the building.

"I'll have a water with lemon, please." I kept flipping through the menu being impressed by the options. I started to feel like Dame was either pressed for some pussy or he was really feeling me. I hope his motives were the second option. By the end of the night, I'd find out the answer to this question.

"So, from your accent I can tell you're not from North Carolina. What brought you down to the dirty-dirty south?" He cracked up laughing at his own corny joke.

"First off, I didn't know North Carolina was considered the dirty south. I'm from Memphis, Tennessee, and I came down here to go to school. Charlotte is the new and upcoming ATL, and the traffic here is perfect for owning my own business one day."

"Looks like I'm sitting in the presence of one of Charlotte's upcoming future entrepreneurs."

This nigga was really laying it on thick with the compliments and shit. "Yeah, something like that. So, what dreams are you trying to fulfill through JCSU?"

"Honestly, I'm hoping to get drafted into the NBA. In the meantime, my backup plan is to get my degree in Sports Management to work with athletes in the leagues if my true dreams of being a baller don't pan out."

"Nice, so I'm sitting in the presence of the next number one draft pick." I smirked as I used his same compliment to compliment him back.

The chemistry between us was undeniable, I felt like I'd known him for so long. Dame was the nigga that every guy wanted to be, and every girl wanted to date, but he didn't act that way. He was cool, instead of cocky. He was chill instead of trying to do the most. He was a breath of fresh air at the time, seeing as most college niggas aren't trying to date or be a one-woman man.

Dame and I had a great vibe going on when the waiter reminded us for the second time that the restaurant would be closing soon. We were so into each other that it didn't feel like damn near two hours had passed since we had arrived and been seated.

Dame grew tired of the waitresses' annoying antics to get us to leave. He took care of the bill and drove us out to the boardwalk for a romantic walk near the water.

There was one question that had been running through my mind since our first encounter that I was dying to ask him. "So, what's the real reason you took me on a date? If you think I'm going to pop it off just because you're a star athlete, then you've got another thing coming," I spoke with pure confidence.

"Woah, Cherish. I don't know what you've heard about me, but if I wanted to just fuck you then I would have said that. I have hoes lined up in my DM's, and seeing as you're in the position that most of them dream of being in, you should know and realize I want more than sex *from you. You're beautiful, busting your ass working, and getting a degree. I respect that. You have a genuine vibe, and I'm hoping you'll give me the opportunity to make you my girl."*

I was prepared for him to give me a bullshit ass answer, but his response was far from it. Hearing Dame say he wanted me to be his girl stirred up butterflies in my stomach and made me blush a little bit, showing off my right dimple.

After Dame checked my ass and made it known that I wasn't just another female on his hit list, I was able to relax. We stayed out till midnight, talking about everything and nothing at all. I learned Dame desired to co-own part of an NBA team one day. He had big dreams which is something I admired about him.

This vibe between the two of us was indescribable. In my twenty-one years of living, nothing ever felt as real as this moment felt with him.

Chapter 1

It Was All Good a Year Ago

Cherish Wright

May 2018

"Love, love, love, love, 'long as we got,

Love, love, love, oh, 'long as we got,

Done with these niggas, I don't love these niggas,

I dust off these niggas, do it for fun,

Don't take it personal, personally,

I'm surprised you called me after the things I said..."

Sza was singing the hell out of her smash hit *"Love Galore"* as I swayed my hips to the beat of the music. Sza was in town for her CTRL tour, and my best friend convinced me to go the concert. I found myself getting lost in the lyrics and remembering all the times I told myself, "Don't fall in love with these niggas". Unfortunately, no matter how much I told myself that, being a hopeless romantic took over my heart every time.

"Cherish, this concert is bomb.com. I'm so glad you decided to step out the house for once and have some fun."

I felt a nasty attitude settling in. "Bitch, please! Just because I don't like to be out every weekend shaking my ass on random niggas doesn't mean I don't like to have fun. There's more to life than twerking."

Before Brittish could come up with a better clap back, Sza started singing *"The Weekend"* and the crowd went crazy. Although I was enjoying myself or at least trying to, this concert really had me in my feelings about Dame.

It had been three months since Dame and I made it official. All the girls on campus often gave me a look of envy whenever we would be out and about together. To my surprise, Dame had showed me and these hoes that he was a one-woman man. It was a typical Friday night, and I was where I usually was sitting in the gym cheering for Dame. You know, being a supportive girlfriend.

It's the second half of the game, and John C. Smith was down by two points with thirteen seconds left. One of Dame's teammates was wasting too much time holding the ball, when he finally decided to throw the ball to Dame. With five seconds left on the clock and the team needing three points to win the game, I knew that's what Dame was aiming for. Dame threw the ball in the air, as I prayed he didn't fuck up this shot. Dame would be in a fucked-up state of mind if this shot cost the team a chance of advancing to the NCAA tournament. The buzzer went off, and the crowd went wild when Dame successfully shot a three-pointer, ultimately winning the game and sending the team to the next division for the NCAA.

I ran out on the court as everybody was cheering and doing a celebratory dance. "Congratulations, babe."

He picked me up, and I wrapped my legs around his waist placing my arms around his neck as we engaged in a passionate kiss. "Nigga, are you gonna play kissy face all night or celebrate with your team?"

Dame's coach questioned. Dame stopped kissing me long enough to inform his coach he'd be going out with the team. I gave him one final tonguing down to remind him of what he already had and told him to enjoy himself tonight.

For some reason, those passionate kisses with Dame did something to me. My roommate was gone for the weekend, so tonight was the perfect opportunity.

I sent Dame a text around eleven p.m., telling him that I had a surprise for him once his little outing with the team was over. I had lit some apple cinnamon candles and put on a red bralette and thong set I had found in my drawer from Victoria Secret.

Minutes after the clock read midnight, I heard a knock at the door, and sure enough, it was Dame. I turned on "Rich Sex" by Future and slipped on my silk robe and black heels. I opened the door slightly for Dame to hear the music and walk in without seeing me in my outfit. I quickly closed the door behind me as he turned around to face me.

"Babe, what's going on?" he asked with a smirk on his face.

I walked closer to him while I was undoing my robe and said, "This is all for you, daddy!" as my robe dropped to the floor.

I walked Dame over to the chair near my desk, and I straddled my legs across his lower body. "You played your heart out tonight, plus you've been hella good to me without begging for some pussy. You're one of the most wanted men on campus, and I know girls still try to hook up with you. This is my way of saying thank you for respecting me and our relationship.".

"Baby, let's go and have rich sex, make a little love on the rich sex," Future sung smoothly as the real action was about to go down.

He picked me up, laid me down, and stripped down to just his boxers. I knew Dame was blessed from all the times I sat on his lap, but the bulge in his boxers made me question if I could handle all of him. He took my heels off and proceeded to place kisses all over my body. He unsnapped my bra giving my nipples a soft pinch as he kissed and gave each breast an even amount of attention. Dame continued to place kisses down my tummy and parted my legs just enough for him to stick his head in between them, placing a kiss on my clit. I could instantly feel my juices soaking up my panties. He pushed my thong to the side placing two fingers in my wetness. "Tight, wet, and shaved. Just how I like it," he stated as he removed his fingers and went in for the kill.

He sucked and licked on my pussy like it was his last supper. His head game was too vicious to the point that I am crying out, "Dameee, I can't take no more I'm about to cum.... shitttt!". All he said was, "Get your first nut off, baby," as my pussy let out a loud farting noise.

Before I could fully recover from my first orgasm, Dame was trying to slide his nine-inch pipe into my throbbing pussy.

"Dame, it's too deep, I can't take it."

"Babe, I barely got the tip in, just trust me, I got you." He attempted to ease more of his dick inside of me. After a few strokes, my honeypot adjusted to his length and width. He grabbed both of my legs and put them on his shoulder, while he was knee deep, swimming inside my love box.

"Shit babe, your pussy is gripping the hell out of my dick." His facial expression formed into a sexy ass fuck face.

To show him the true magic of my lovebox, I started contracting my muscles which caused him to grunt loud as fuck. I swear the way we were getting down between the sheets, I knew this was going to be a forever thing between us.

Out of nowhere, he looked me square in my eyes and said, "I love you, Cherish, always and forever." Hearing that he loved me made another orgasm creep up in my stomach.

"I ooo weee...love you too, baby!" I said while being in a state of euphoria.

I don't know if it was because my honeypot was that good or what, but that was the first time we said, "I love you" to each other. I prayed to God he really meant it; this man is everything I've dreamed of plus more.

✳✳✳

Nine months passed by, and today was Dame and I's one-year anniversary. In honor of celebrating, Dame made reservations at Fahrenheit. I'd been feinding to go to this place. My baby knew how to listen to my wants and make sure he satisfied my needs.

"Cherish, hurry up. We have reservations at eight, and you know traffic is hectic down I-40."

"I'm almost ready, babe. Let me grab my heels."

Twenty minutes later, we're pulling up to the restaurant and being seated at our table. This place looked even more beautiful in person than it did online. The roof top scenery, downtown lighting, and the fire pits were perfect for tonight's occasion.

"Bae, I don't know what to get. Everything on the menu looks delicious."

"Get whatever," was all Dame could say before his cell phone started ringing. I started to remind him of the no phone policy while we're on dates, but he had already answered the call. I could tell by his comments and facial expressions this phone call was serious. A few minutes passed by before Dame wrapped up his phone call.

"Babe, that was my coach, and guess who just got offered an NBA deal?"

"OH, MY GOD! Dameee, that's amazing." I jumped up to give him a hug. Instead of him embracing it, he had a sad look on his face.

"Babe, get excited, your dreams of making it into the NBA just came true!" I exclaimed with a confused look on my face. All Dame talks about is making it to the big leagues. Now the opportunity is here, he's not as happy as I envisioned him being.

"I don't know how to say this, Cherish, but the deal is for playing overseas in Italy."

I felt like my heart had stopped beating. I never in a million years gave it a thought that he would get offered a deal overseas. I just assumed his deal would be with the Charlotte Hornets since that's where he lived and played college ball for. An uneasy feeling crept up in my stomach, and a lump in my throat formed as I forced myself to say "So, what does this mean for us?"

I know I sounded selfish, but Dame and I were perfect together, and everything I longed for was going to be more than a twelve-hour plane ride away. Not to mention the foreign bitches throwing themselves at him.

"Truthfully, I don't know what this means for us. I want to say we'll make things work, but we're still young. We're about to graduate in a few weeks. I mean, I'm only twenty-two, and maybe after my contract is up, I'll get a deal playing in the states."

Tears began to flow from my eyes as I came to realize this was his awful way of saying goodbye.

***

"Girl, I know your ass ain't cryin'. Sza's lyrics is hittin' you that deep, sis?" Brittish fished through her purse to hand me a tissue. Honestly, I didn't realize I had shed a few tears until Brittish snapped me back to reality.

"Girl, it's just my allergies acting up again." I attempted to clear up my face.

"Are you sure you're okay, sis? I'm sorry for buying tickets to this concert. I should've known attending a SZA event would've been too much for you. Actually, we can leave early if you want oo." Brittish started getting her stuff together.

"No, it's cool, Brittish, I'm good. I promise. I'm going to the bathroom to freshen up, and I'll be back".

Truthfully, the minute I closed the bathroom stall door, I broke down crying. I missed him, and I felt so stupid every time I started crying about this shit. On top of that, now Brittish was going to suspect I wasn't over him yet. No matter how much I swore up and down I didn't miss him anymore, my two besties always knew I was lying.

At times I felt like I was ready to move on such as a few months ago when I tried to date again. Sadly, every time I was with this new guy, all I did was compare him to Dame. In true nigga fashion, he dropped my ass quick and told me to call him when I'd let go of the past.

This last year was nothing like I thought it would be. I dreamed that Dame and I were going to ride off into the sunset with talks of wedding bells within the next few years. I thought I was going to be loving my career and received a promotion, but boy was I completely wrong. I've spent majority of the last year crying and being alone, but I'm starting to grow tired of that lifestyle. I'm twenty-three years young and a college graduate with my entire life ahead of me. It's time to stop acting like a weak ass bitch and get back on my boss shit. These were going to be the last tears I shed over the past as I dabbed my eyes dry.

Knock! Knock! "Cherish, it's me, please open the door. I'm here for you and I'm fine with us leaving." I could hear Brittish pleading on the other side of the stall door.

I unlocked the door and brushed passed her to fix my makeup in the mirror. "Listen sis, I had a moment. I'm good now, and I'll forever be good moving forward. Don't keep apologizing for something that wasn't your fault. Let's enjoy the rest of the concert and put this sad ass moment behind us." My stern voice let her know this conversation was a wrap.

I ran a comb through my hair, did a once over in the mirror, and headed back to our seats for the rest of the concert. I returned in the nick of time as SZA sung her final song *"Broken Clocks"* which happens to be my favorite song on the album. She shut The Cone Denim Theater down with another banger.

My spirits were backed lifted, and I didn't feel like going back to Brittish's place just yet. "Sis, let's go to Limelight for the after party; I heard it's going to be lit." I nudged Brittish in her side wondering if she heard me through the noisy crowd.

"You know I'm always ready to shake this romp," Brittish responded back as she made her ass clap in a black sequin BCBG romper that fit her ass to a tee.

∗∗∗

As I was driving downtown looking for a parking spot, my left hand, better known as Kenly, was calling my phone.

"Hey hoe, I've been calling you since I got into town this morning, and your ass is just now calling me back." I busted a right at the stoplight.

"Girl, I've been busy working, and it slipped my mind that you were coming into town today. Sorry, love. I was hoping we could grab a bite to eat tomorrow before you leave."

"Of course, you know my country bama ass ain't missin' no meals. You should get dressed and pop out tonight. Brittish and I decided to hit up Limelight for the Sza afterparty."

"Lord, best friend, you should have told me that earlier before I made plans to go out on a date with this guy I met on Instagram."

I love my best friend and all, but she stays doing some risky shit such as meeting a guy off the internet. "Kenly, why the fuck are you going on a date with a stranger?"

I knew this conversation was about to go left. Kenly and I rarely saw eye to eye on relationships. I remember when Dame and I broke up, her dumb ass had the nerve to say he could fly me out, and things would remain the same. Yes, it's true, he could've flown me out to Italy, but our relationship would have been far from the same after he entered the league. Kenly has always been too carefree and optimistic with giving love a try.

"Because I'm grown, and last time I checked, my mama isn't Cherish Wright. Just because you don't plan to remove the cob webs on your pussy doesn't mean the rest of us aren't trying to enjoy life," Kenly responded nastily.

That was a low blow for Kenly to say some shit like that. She knows better than anyone outside of Brittish what I've been through. I was ready to go in on her when Brittish said, *"Kenly, you're dead wrong for saying that shit. Send us your location for this date in case something happens to you."*

Before Brittish could utter another word, I pressed a black button on my steering wheel disconnecting the call. If I planned to enjoy my night, dwelling on the bullshit Kenly just said wasn't a good way to kick off the evening. After a few minutes of riding in silence, I whipped my car into a parking spot.

Brittish reached in the backseat for her tan Coco Chanel purse to search for something. "You want some of this Crown Royal, before we get out of the car? It might help you loosen up and pull some fine ass niggas tonight." She opened the fresh bottle of brown liquor, taking a sip from the bottle.

This chick was the only person I know that always had liquor on deck. No matter what, you could count on Brittish to have a small flask or bottle nearby. The same way true smokers keep a blunt stashed away, Brittish was the same way with alcohol. She wasn't an alcoholic by any means, but she loved to get lit.

"Nah, I'm good, boo. If I get fucked up, how are we going to get home tonight? You know I'm not leaving my baby in this parking lot overnight, and as far as rekindling my love life, we'll see about that. I don't think Usher was serious when he wrote *"Love in this Club."* Brittish couldn't stop laughing, and the baby that I was referring to is my 2017 all black Lexus IS 250. I worked too hard for my baby to be left in an unsecured parking lot.

"Damn, you're right. I know how you are about your most prized possession. That only means more liquor for meee," she sang, downing some Crown Royal.

I knew tonight was bound to be interesting. Brittish was going to be bent while I adjusted to the club scene. This was my first-time partying or doing anything fun in over six months. When Dame left, I was in and out of a depressive state of mind where I went to work and back home to sulk at my lonely apartment. I'm grateful my friends and family tolerated me during one of the lowest moments of my life.

I stepped out of the car and hit the lock button, as we found our way to the club entrance.

The club line was long as fuck, and I was willing to pay whatever for the VIP line. Plus, Brittish and I looked too fly to be waiting in line with hoes that looked like their outfits came from the thrift store. I wore a blush pink bodycon dress from Garb Boutique that hugged my curves with a pair of nude Steve Madden heels, while Brittish was dressed in designer too. After ten minutes in the VIP line, the security guard checked our ID's, patted us down, and opened the door to the club. It was packed as hell in this bitch, but that's to be expected as the concert afterparty and regular club goers were all attending the same event.

Hearing the trap music booming through the building while the familiar scent of liquor and booty sweat lightened my mood. I can't believe I've let so much time go by without living life. I could tell by the way my ass started bouncing in tune with the beat as we maneuvered through the building that I had to start going out more often. Although I was against drinking moments ago, the club vibe was too enticing not to drink, just a little bit. I grabbed Brittish's hand heading towards the bar.

As we waited for the bartender to take our order, Brittish tapped me on my shoulder to say, "I think that guy is checking you out." I glanced over to where I felt the stares coming from, and some tall, dark-skinned gentleman was gazing at me. I couldn't make out his facial features since the atmosphere was dark with low lighting, but from afar, he looked handsome. My eyes finally met his, but I quickly looked away to avoid a stare down. I wasn't shy, but like I said earlier, I'm not hoping to find love in this club.

"Damnnnn bitch, he's feeling you!" Brittish said loud and slowly as she held onto my arm for dear life, indicating she was drunk already. I waved off Brittish's comment, but I could still feel his eyes on me.

The bartender came down to our end of the bar to take our orders, and against my better judgement, I let Brittish order a drink. Minutes later, I was sipping on a Sex on the Beach with an extra shot, and Brittish was enjoying her Blue Motorcycle. Brittish was bopping her head and imitating how rappers act when they're jumping around performing, causing me to bust out laughing.

"Bitch, what are you laughing at? You know these young rappers be dancin' and actin' a fool on stage," Brittish mentioned while she finished her drink.

"Girl, you're a mess. I'm so glad you talked me into visiting you. I know I've been down in the dumps this last year, but I'm going to do better."

"Cherish, you're my best friend. The yin to my yang. The peanut butter to my jelly. My partner in crime. I'm always going to be here for you, no matter what. Through the good and the bad, this friendship is down to ride till the very end."

My lips formed into a smile, showing my pearly white teeth and dimple. I gave Brittish a big hug. Without my two best friends, I don't know how I would've made it through the turmoil.

"Alright sis, the sappy moment is over. Let's explore the rest of the club. It's three stories, and each level is playing a different genre of music. Hence, the first level is playing trap rap."

The first level of the club was cool, but I was more than ready to listen to something else. Trap music tends to bring out the ratchetness in people, however, I was in the mood to throw my ass in a circle. I held my drink in my left hand and held Brittish's hand even tighter with my free hand as we took the stairs to the second level.

This level was packed to capacity since twerk music was playing. There were half naked dancers on the stage and bottle girls serving the VIP section. Brittish and I took a seat at a vacant black booth near the dance floor. As I took in the atmosphere, I could sense somebody was looking at me again.

My eyes danced around the club to see who was gazing at me, and there he was. My eyes met his again, only this time I could get a better look at his face. He was indeed as handsome as I thought with dark brown piercing eyes. I immediately started blushing and tensed up as I realized he was walking towards me.

This fine chocolate gentleman smoothly approached me. "My name is Aaron, but most people call me Ace. I've had my eyes on you all night. It is a pleasure to be meeting the most gorgeous woman in the building. Let me buy you a drink and get to know you better?"

I was pondering on how I should answer his question. This man was bold enough to follow me to the second floor, approach me while my homegirl is sitting here, and offered to buy me a drink. I was slightly impressed with his desire to talk to me.

Before I could answer, Brittish quickly interrupted by saying, "Yes" and took off towards the dance floor, leaving me alone with this fine ass stranger. He stared at me waiting for me to confirm the answer that Brittish gave him. I extended my hand and introduced myself as he helped me get up from the open booth I was sitting in. This man was being a true gentleman. Umph, I wonder how long this act was going to last. He used his left hand to motion for me to start walking ahead of him. "Ladies first."

I gracefully sashayed over to the bar doing the Naomi Campbell walk, that one drink had me feeling myself. One of the bottle girls approached us and gave me the evil eye before she asked for our order. I figured she was another hating ass bitch since I've never seen this chick a day before in my life.

"I'll have two shots of Jack Daniels, no chaser," I asked for boldly. Although I'm not a heavy drinker, I needed something intense that would loosen me up. Being in Aaron's presence was making me nervous. He ordered something light which was a Corona and paid for our drinks.

He made a remark when I took my first shot straight to the head. "I see you're drinking the strong liquor tonight."

"I like my liquor how I like my men, strong and dark," I replied before I downed my second shot. I was lying through my teeth knowing Dame was light-skinned, but this was my way of flirting. I wanted Aaron to know off bat the type of woman he was trying to deal with.

"You didn't strike me as a heavy drinker, but it looks like the odds are in your favor, I'm strong and dark. I mean, they do say the blacker the berry, the sweeter the juice." He gave me a cocky look with his dark brown eyes.

As I stared back at him, his eyes won me over. Ugh, I've always been a sucker for pretty eyes. A person's eyes can tell me a great deal about their soul. His eyes read that he was cool, yet mysterious, which made me feel unsure about him. As the liquor settled in, I pushed my apprehensive thoughts to the back of my mind and started moving my hips to *"Booty"* by Blac Youngsta.

I grabbed his hand leading us to the dance floor. His hands caressed my hips as I twerked my ass and threw it back on him a few times. To my surprise, he could keep up with me, and our bodies were in sync with each other's. Out of nowhere, I heard Brittish's loud ass mouth saying "FUCKKK IT UP, SIS!". I can always count on her to be my hype man. I continued to throw my ass back like my life depended on it.

A part of me wondered why I was going so hard in the club for a guy I just met five minutes ago, but I desperately needed this moment. It was my way of proving to myself, my friends, and anybody else that Cherish was moving on. I twerked to the next two songs before my ass needed a break.

Aaron wiped beads of sweat off his forehead. "Damn girl, you worked a nigga out."

"Nigga please, I can tell you work out. I know damn well those three songs didn't affect you. If anything, the arch in my back is the one that got a workout," I stated while gently massaging my lower back.

"If you were my girl, I'd give you a workout every night."

I felt slightly uncomfortable yet turned on at the thought of him giving me a workout in the bedroom. I'd barely known this man for a night, yet I was thinking about him sexually. I knew I needed some dick but not from a random stranger at the club.

I needed to dead this situation and quick, "Listen, I'm enjoying myself but I'm not looking for anything serious. I'm only in town until tomorrow."

"I'm not trying to pressure you into doing nothing right now. Let's go to the third level, they're playing R&B music." He led me to the last and final floor of the club.

I tried to look around for Brittish as we walked towards the stairs, but I couldn't find her. I figured she was somewhere in the building dancing her ass off. I wasn't too worried about her because she was a partier, but she had a man that would jack her up if he heard she was out here wilding out. I figured sending her a text of my whereabouts with Aaron would be enough until we linked back up.

A breeze of wind hit my face as we made it to the third floor which was the rooftop. It was beautiful, you could see the city lights, and the view was perfect of downtown Greensboro. I liked this level the most as it was quiet and not nearly as populated as the other two floors. The classic slow jam *"I Want to Be Your Man"* was playing when he used the opportunity to wrap his arms around my waist.

He whispered in my ear, "Am I holding you too tightly?"

I quickly responded back, "No, you're holding me perfectly." It'd been over a year since I'd shared such an intimate moment with a man. I damn near forgot how good it felt to be held. Nothing can measure up to a manly man's touch.

Although I told him I didn't want nothing serious, everything about this moment felt right. The music, the way he held me, and the comfortableness I felt in his arms were all the elements that were making me wish this moment could last forever. Ugh, I was feeling conflicted between my intuition telling me to leave this man alone and my heart feeling opened to the thought of dating again.

✳✳✳

Aaron and I were coupled up in a corner on the rooftop, embracing the scenery and music when my phone dinged notifying me I had a text.

Brittish: *Where are you at? I'm ready to leave.*

Me: *I'm on the third floor, I'll meet you at the front entrance.*

Ugh, I knew the night was bound to end soon, but I wanted tonight to last a little longer. Against my wishes, I told Aaron, "I truly enjoyed myself tonight thanks to you, but my homegirl is ready to go."

He grabbed my face and placed a delicate kiss on my cheek. "I enjoyed you too, put my number in your phone. I want to see you again whether that means I'm coming to you, or you're coming back to my city. I know you're not looking for nothing serious, but I always get what I want, which is you." The night was going well until his arrogance started to show.

No matter what I said to defer him from being uninterested in me, he didn't let up on his approach, and he felt the need to give me a nickname already, which was Chocolate. This nigga was really trying it.

"I understand you normally get what you want, but in the words of Beyoncé, come harder, this won't be easy," I replied with a smirk on my face. I think it's cute that he's smitten with me, but it's also a turn off that he's cocky and arrogant.

"I hear what you're saying, but I'm a man of my word. I love a good chase if it means I win the prize. Take my number, and whenever you're ready, we can link up."

This moment felt like déjà vu. Aaron isn't the first guy and probably won't be the last to take an interest in me. However, curiosity got the best of me which is why I gave him my gold iPhone 8 to save his number. He gave me my phone back, and I was prepared to walk away when he said, "A nigga can't get no love before you dip out?"

I turned around and gave him a one arm hug. I took in his scent and physique for the last time, knowing the chances of seeing him again were slim to none, although he had every intention on seeing me again. A long-distance relationship never interested me. If it did, I would have made things work with Dame. The hug lingered on longer than I cared for it too, but I finally pulled away and made a bee line for the exit door.

It took a minute getting to the entrance with everybody traveling up and down the staircase. Once I saw the double doors to the entrance, I peeped Brittish sitting on the floor with her heels in her hand, looking a mess. I wished I would've kept a better eye on her.

"Woah Britt, I leave you for two hours, and you look like you got ran over by a dump truck." I couldn't contain myself from laughing my ass off.

"Bitchhh, now is not the time for jokes. I'm ready to go, and if I knew Grant... wouldn't be mad at me, I would've calleddd... him to come pick me up." Brittish slurred. I looked at her once more and decided pulling the car up would be easier than dragging her ass there.

"Hang tight, boo. I'm going to pull up the car, then we'll be heading home."

I stared at Aaron's contact info while I walked to the car. I wasn't sure if I'd ever reach out to him, but I'm grateful tonight happened. I was brought out of the sad slump I've been in for quite some time. For this reason alone, it felt amazing to know I was getting my groove back.

Chapter 2

Back to life...Back to reality

Kenly

"Hello, I called a few minutes ago and made a reservation under Thomas for a group of three," I mentioned to the hostess at Tripp's. A couple of minutes passed by before I was seated.

"Can I get you something to drink or an appetizer while we wait for the others to get here?" asked the young lady.

"Sure, I'll have a strawberry margarita and an order of mild buffalo wings," I requested while I continued to look through the menu.

Let me introduce myself. My name is Kenly Thomas, and I've been best friends with Cherish and Brittish since the college days. We met each other at freshman orientation and immediately cliqued. I remember the night we met like it was yesterday. We were attending the freshman orientation mixer in the commons area of the residence hall. A DJ, residential advisor, and ton of high school seniors that were ready to be grown, flooded the vicinity. While everybody was dancing to the music, I was posted up against the wall, and Cherish was a few feet away from me doing the same thing. Most people thought I was acting stuck up, but I was just keeping to myself until I saw some females that seemed like good people.

Out of nowhere, this random girl who later turned out to be Brittish, came over trying to dance on me and ultimately pulled

Cherish and I into the crowd. We danced and talked to a few other incoming freshmen for a little bit. Brittish was truly the life of the party, mingling and dancing with everybody. This was one of the many things I admired and noticed how her spirit kept everybody else going.

The night after the party, Brittish saw Cherish and me sitting as loners during breakfast, so she invited us to come eat with her. I took this opportunity as the chance to make friends since I never had true girlfriends in high school. During breakfast, I learned a lot about these two, and we've been ride or die for each other ever since.

Speaking of these hoes, let me call them to see where they're at. Before I could finish dialing Cherish's number, I could hear her voice at the front of the restaurant telling the host she already had a table. Within minutes, my two besties were joining me at a booth near the back side of the restaurant.

Cherish was all smiles and greeted me in a sweet angelic tone. "Ken, you're looking gorgeous as always. I missed you, girl." I wore a pair of Fashion Nova ripped jeans with a burnt orange top that showed off my flat tummy and some nude Steven Madden heels. My orange top coordinated perfectly with my caramel skin complexion. If I must say so myself, I was dressed to the nines today.

It took me by surprise that she was still happy to see me after the comment I said to her last night. Cherish and I have a love-hate relationship. We love each other to death, but we often have our spats over the pettiest shit.

"Thanks boo, I've missed you, and you look stunning too. I see you've dropped some more weight."

Cherish started eating her feelings after the breakup which naturally led to several pounds being added on. It was good to see she kept her promise of living a healthier lifestyle. I greeted and hugged Brittish too. She looked tired as hell which meant she partied hard last night. Between the three of us, Brittish has always been the calm, supportive, turn up friend. She never let the petty drama bother her, and she knew how to listen without being judgmental. At times I envied that she lived a peaceful life with minimum bullshit. In my world, some shit was always popping off.

"Y'all let me tell you about this blind date I went on. So, this nigga was fine as hell from his Instagram pictures. He was dark-skinned with a close haircut and a full Rick Ross beard. Tell me why when I see him in person, he looked like Kodak Black. I was highly disappointed to say the least. Then, his card got declined when he tried to pay for dinner. I paid for it and made sure to block his broke bum ass." I started getting pissed off again as I recalled the epic date I should've have never gone on.

"Well, all I'm going to say is I told your ass not to go on a blind date, but you never listen to me. Maybe this will teach you to get off that online dating shit," Cherish stated as she grabbed one of my buffalo wings. I should've known she'd have something to say. At times, I truly felt like she wants us to be single just because she chooses not to be on the dating scene. I understood that heartbreak had taken its toll on my best friend, but damn, that didn't mean the rest of us had to be scared to love.

I rolled my eyes deciding that arguing with her right now wasn't necessary since I hadn't seen her in months. The waitress came back at the perfect moment to take our order and grab the menus off the table.

"Cherish what's been going on in the 704? We haven't gotten together in a while," Brittish asked with a raised eyebrow.

"Girl, ain't nothing happening in Charlotte but me taking my country bama ass to work. I'm trying to get promoted to branch manager."

We all graduated a little over a year ago from JCSU and landed us some grown women jobs. Cherish got her business degree with a concentration in accounting and started working for Wells Fargo's corporate office as a recruiter. However, Brittish and I received a degree in Biology. We both were offered jobs in Greensboro where I started working as a chemist and Brittish became a laboratory technician. As you see, we can't get together like we used to back in the day. We've bossed up and became some money hungry females.

In the midst of reminiscing about the college days ,I blurted out, "Cherish, you should look for a position in Greensboro. I mean, you don't have any family or anybody special there anymore. This is a nice city, and you'll be closer to your girls."

"Honestly, I've considered that already. It's too many memories I'm steady trying to forget about in Charlotte. I do miss having you guys around, and Greensboro is somewhat closer to Memphis. I'm thinking about talking to the director of human resources to see if any positions or promotions are available in the area."

"Yessss, sis! The 336 ain't ready for the Fab Three to take over the city." Brittish let out a playful laugh. The Fab Three was our crew nickname, like the ladies in Girl's Trip calling themselves Flossy Possy.

I was beaming from the inside out at the thought of the whole crew being in the same city again. Like I said before, Cherish and I have our disagreements, but my life wouldn't be complete without my left hand by my side.

Cherish

Knock. Knock. I heard a soft tap on my office door. "Come in," I said.

"Ms. Wright, Jared Daniels is here for his interview," said the front desk assistant.

"Thank you, Tori. Can you print out his resume and walk him down to the conference room?"

It'd been two weeks since I got promoted as branch manager for the main office in the Greensboro district. All interviewees were interviewed by me, and after a successful second interview with HR and a background check, I could place them at one of the stores in the area. Initially, I was nervous about leaving Charlotte, but I'm loving my new job position. I gathered the materials I needed to host an interview before I headed down to the conference room.

"Hello Mr. Daniels, I'm Ms. Wright…. the branch manager of this location and district manager of the Guilford county region. It's a pleasure to meet you." I extended my right hand out to him. I barely finished my introduction before my hands started sweating suddenly. I've had the proper training and handled a few interviews already, but this fine specimen standing in front of me had me off my game.

Greensboro was a city full of handsome black men. This was the fifth guy I've seen in this week that looked like God took his time creating him. Jared stood at five-foot-nine inches, light-skinned, and grey colored eyes. He resembled the rapper J. Cole, but without the crazy hair. He sported a close fade and had some pearly white teeth. You could tell he worked out from the way his muscles showed through his business attire.

I didn't realize I had been shaking his hand for a while until he said, "You have a firm handshake," snapping me out of the daze that I was in.

I wiped my sweaty palms on my yellow pencil skirt. "My apologies, I got distracted for a moment. Take a seat. I'm going to show you a PowerPoint about the teller position before we begin the interview."

I managed to get through the five-minute presentation without getting drawn into his physique. "I've told you some valuable information about the company and the position you applied for. Can you tell me a little bit about yourself?"

***

Thankfully, twenty minutes later, the interview was coming to an end. I was in and out of daydreaming for the most part, but I heard him say he was twenty-six-years-old, with previous bank experience.

"Thank you for coming in today. As I said earlier, it was a pleasure to meet you-" I barely finished my statement before he cut me off. "The pleasure was all mine," he said in a deep baritone voice. If I didn't know any better, I would assume he was flirting with me.

"I'm meeting with the rest of the HR team later this week, and you'll hear back from us if we decide to have a second interview."

We shook hands again, but this time, I kept minimal eye contact with him. He had a firm grip on my hand. "I know this isn't professional, but you're a beautiful lady."

Lord knows if only I believed in mixing business with pleasure, he could certainly have his way with me right now in this room. It's been over a year since I've had sex. It's safe to say I'm sex deprived. Changing from getting it in on the regular to going cold turkey was tough as nails. However, the way these men are looking in the 336, I don't know if I'll be able to hold out much longer.

I cleared my throat and slowly removed my hand from his grasp. "Let me walk you out." I tilted my head away from him trying to disguise how tempted I was feeling.

It seemed liked I couldn't reach the waiting area soon enough. I needed some space between the two of us, immediately. I handed Tori his paperwork and made small talk with her until he got on the elevator. I took one last look at him as he winked at me before the elevator doors started to close.

"Oooouuuu, somebody is into you, Ms. Wright," Tori announced.

"Whatever, ain't nobody checkin' for him." I waved off the comment.

"Well, it looks like he's definitely checking for you."

For some reason, I found myself getting worked up for various reasons after Jared left. I keep saying I'm ready to move on, but every time a guy approached me, it was under the wrong circumstances, such as, Jared was finger -icking good, but I would never date a potential employee, and that guy from the club was too cocky for my liking. I let out a deep sigh as I realized I let all that fineness walk away from me.

"Tori, I'm taking an early lunch break. If somebody calls for me, forward them to my voicemail."

I made it to my office, locked the door, and searched through my desk drawer for my nine-inch pink jack rabbit dildo I called Dee. Dee was the first name that popped into my head the night I bought my toy from Adam and Eve. He was the truth, with seven different speeds, waterproof, and the front had a vibrator attached to it for stimulating the clitoris. I know it's inappropriate to bring my toy to the workplace, but a girl has needs, and right now, I needed to take care of those needs. I kept a dildo at work and at home for times like this when I needed an immediate release.

I turned up the music playing on Pandora, sliding down my black lace panties. I leaned back a bit in my rolling chair and placed my left foot at the end of the seat leaving room for me to have access to my slit. I massaged my clit while rubbing the dildo up and down my honeypot. Thoughts of Jared and the nasty things he would do to me flooded my mind as I pushed the plastic dick inside of me inch by inch. I turned the speed of the dildo up to the max, as my body went into a state of ecstasy.

Chapter 3

We Meet Again

Aaron (Ace)

"Aye Trina, get yo' ass up. It's time for you to bounce." I was irritated as hell this morning. Of course, her ass started whining and said, "Why are you kicking me out so soon?" I wanted to slap her for questioning me, but I realized a potential assault isn't something I needed on my squeaky-clean record.

"I told you I had things to do today. It's ten in the morning, and I'm already behind schedule from fucking around with your ass. As of today, no more spending the night. We fuck, and you bounce. You're starting to get too comfortable with staying the night and shit." I know I sounded like an asshole, but Trina was supposed to be a hit it and quit it type of deal. This situation had lasted long enough.

Trina was a fine ass light-skinned shorty I met through one of my homies. She was good in bed and a great person to accompany me to different work events. As a business man, it's only right I showed up with a pretty lady on my arm. If I keep her laced in designer and bought those expensive ass bundles she loves to wear, she was pleased with the state of our relationship. Most people thought we had a good thing going since she didn't pressure a nigga for a title, but I wanted something more that Trina just didn't offer if I was seriously going to settle down one day and start a family. Trina was a good girl, but she wasn't going to be my future. Being wifey material was completely different from being one of my go to women.

Trina let out a long huff and threw the covers back over her head. I snatched the covers back exposing her naked body, throwing her shirt at her. "If you know what's best for you, you'll be out of my condo by the time I get out of the shower."

I wrapped a towel around my waist and opened the door to let the steaming hot air out. I walked past my bedroom to reach my closet being satisfied with Trina's disappearance, she knew I meant business.

I searched through the closet looking for a chill yet sophisticated ensemble. I settled for a pair of True Religion blue jeans, an all-black Versace polo with Versace written in white letters on the shoulders, and black Jordan retro's 13. I was ready to hit the streets of Greensboro and handle some work business.

My first stop was the barbershop. As a business man, I always needed to look the part, and getting a shape up was top priority. I'm the proud co-owner of Ross Trucking Company which I've been running for almost three years now. My dad started this company twenty years ago. He established his own trucking company after being on the road for some years trying to save up enough money to buy a few trucks. His business plan of staying small expanded over the years, and when I graduated from college, he handed down the business to my older brother and me. Since we've taken over the company, we're now located in seven cities across North Carolina, and we're looking to branch out to other states soon. Business has been booming, and I'm forever grateful my pops started a legacy for the Ross family.

I pulled into the shopping center in search of a parking spot near the barbershop when I suddenly had to hit my brakes. A dumb ass broad running her mouth on the phone almost walked in front of my matte grey Audi a6. I was pissed to say the least as I whipped the car into an open space. I quickly shut off the car stepping out to jog up to the clueless female.

She was too deep into her conversation to notice my presence until I blocked her entrance into the building. I had a good mind to cuss her ass out for not watching where she was going until I realized I knew this chick. How could I forget that beautiful chocolate face? This was the same chick I met a few weeks ago at Limelight.

I cleared my throat to gain her attention. She jumped back, almost dropping her phone. She was just as shocked as I was that we had run into each other. "Long time no see, my love," I chuckled with a smirk on my face. I thought I'd never see her pretty ass again.

"Oh, my God, you scared me half to death," she responded as she held her chest to show how startled she felt.

I stepped closer to her and grabbed her chin. "What happened to you hitting me up the next time you're in town? I was dead serious about wanting to see you again."

She rudely removed my hand from her face letting out a long huff under her breath. I could have offended her but being aggressive typically made things go my way.

"Please don't touch my face. I didn't think after having one night of fun, that gave you the right to touch me, let alone question me. I recall telling you I'm not interested in nothing serious. I just moved here, and I have too much going on in my life to check in with strangers," she remarked while rolling her eyes.

Normally, I would have said, "Fuck this bitch, I don't have time for the attitude." However, this attitude of hers was a turn on. She stood her ground and didn't allow me to run over her. "You're a feisty little thing, but I like it. I'm sorry for giving you a hard time. Let me treat you to dinner since I'm still labeled as a stranger." I hope she felt my genuineness, but regardless, I wasn't taking no for an answer.

Some would say I'm being arrogant, but when you're a man of my caliber, you never like to hear the word no.

"Hmmm, nice offer, but I'll pass," she said coldly while trying to walk around me.

"Damn, what a nigga gotta do to get you to say yes? I'll take you to Ruth Chris or wherever your heart desires. The royal treatment will be sponsored by me." I've never been pressed for a female, but everything about her intrigued me. Her chocolate skin was smooth with plump pink lips. Her ass was fat and thighs were as thick as my wallet. Her smile with a dimple was endearing yet her attitude signaled she didn't take nobody's mess. Hands down, baby girl was the shit, she was different.

She twirled her finger in her hair shifting all her weight to her left foot. "Your offer is sweet, but it's still a no for me," she stated with a nice nasty attitude.

This chick was going to be a tough nutshell to crack open, but in due time, I know she'll be begging to be mine.

"You've wasted enough of my time for the day, can you move or at least open the door for me?"

"Sure, I'll get the door for you, but next time, watch where you're going. The next nigga might run your chocolate ass over," I mentioned playfully as I pulled open the glass door.

When she walked through the door, a flashback of her throwing her ass on me flooded my memory. I was tempted to slap her thick ass, but I knew better than to disrespect her in such a way. She looked like the type to fight a nigga for doing some foul mess like that. She headed straight for the nail salon, and I went to the barbershop area.

"I'll be seeing your pretty ass sometime soon," I called out to her before the salon door closed. She turned around flashing me the middle finger. I laughed and ran my hand over my face as I thought about the wild goose chase, she was going to send me on.

I dapped up my barber and took a seat in his chair. I was at this place called Barber Nails and Beyond which was hands down the best barbershop in the 336 area. This location had everything from nails and hair to a tattoo parlor.

"What up, Ace? I see you've got your eyes on your next prey," Ted spoke, dapping me up and getting the clippers to shape me up. The preys he was referring to are the females I seek out to be my girl for the night. I've met some of the baddest chicks in the game while I was getting a cut. Now that I think about it, I hope those nosey ass nail techs don't tell Cherish about my scandalous past. I'm well-known around here, which means rumors are constantly circulating around who I'm currently dating.

"Nah man, she's going to be more than a one-night stand or a come through type of chick."

"Shitting me, I'll believe it when I see it. You've never been tied down to one woman before." Ted placed the black cape around me turning the clippers on.

"True point. It's never too late to switch up and be down for one woman. I got a feeling she'll change a young bachelor like myself." I tugged at my beard. I had my work cut out for me, but in due time, I planned to make shawty mine.

Kenly

"Mmmmm…Jay, I've missed you. Fuck me like you hate me." I hissed while I was riding Jaylen's ten-inch dick in the reverse cowgirl position.

"I'm going to fuck you like I hate you, alright, if I find out you've been seeing other niggas again. I'm the only one that can make this pussy sing," he commanded as my pussy leaked out sweet juices. I knew his comment was referring to the date I went on with that broke bum from IG.

"Is this pussy mine, Ken?" he demanded to know while running his hands through my plum colored hair.

I heard him talking to me, but I was in a sexual trance trying to focus on busting this nut. My hands clinched his thighs, and my nails dug into his skin as I bounced up and down on his dick with my legs resting on both sides of his chest. "Kenly! Kenly! Answer me right now, or I'm pushing you off my dick."

"Yes! Jayyyyy! Yes! This pussy is always going to be yours!" I yelled as my second orgasm released on his meaty dick.

The urge to suck the skin off his manhood and taste my own juices overcame me. I hopped off his meat, sliding my booty back on his chest, and slid his shaft into my moist mouth. I used one hand to keep his dick steady as my head bobbed up and down, while the other hand massaged his balls.

"Suck that dick, Ken. Shitttt!" He grunted as the speed of my slurping and sucking skills increased. I could see his toes curling up, damn, my dick sucking skills were too ruthless.

He placed his hands around my hips, slightly lifting my booty up. Like the real nigga he was, I felt his lips placing sloppy kisses on my pussy, then he used his thick pink tongue to separate the folds to attack my cookie.

This was an epic sixty-nine position. "Get ready, Ken, I'm about to cum." I pulled his dick out of my mouth just before he started shooting off everywhere. Everybody knows black girls don't swallow. Shortly after my disrespectful pussy squirted in his face, completing my second orgasm, I rolled onto my stomach, thinking he managed to get me out of my panties yet again. He went into the bathroom and came back with a warm rag to clean up my snatch. I pulled the covers over my head as self-guilt washed over me.

I promised myself I was going to end this situationship between us. Jaylen had been something like a boyfriend to me over the last year, but he never wanted to commit. Through all the talks, good times, and mind-blowing sex, nothing was good enough for him to call me his girl. I thought I came to terms with the status of our relationship, but I haven't. Being good enough for sex, but not worthy of a title wasn't working for me anymore.

It's crazy how after I busted a nut that I started thinking clear as day. I could hear the shower being turned on as I closed my eyes to contemplate why I still fooled around with him. In the midst of my deep thoughts, Jaylen pulled the covers off me. "Don't fall asleep on me. Let's go for another round in the shower."

I instantly felt myself getting pissed, I was ready to snap. "Does it look like I'm in the mood to give you some more ass? Let me answer that question for you, HELL NO!" I retorted angrily getting out of the bed to search for my robe.

"Why are you tripping? You used to love shower sex." He had a disdained look on his face in disbelief that I finally said no to something.

I rolled my eyes as I debated on whether I should explain my thoughts and feelings once again. "You know what, Jay, I used to love a lot of shit, including you, but things have changed. I want more. Shit, hell, I deserve more than good times between the sheets. I deserve a man who wants to be my everything. Clearly, that man isn't you!"

"Not this shit again. Listen, I like you, and I thought we were building a friendship, then a relationship could be a possibility." He ran his hands over his face, indicating that I was stressing him out.

"Nigga, we been building a friendship for a year now. If you don't know by now that I'm more than worthy of being your girlfriend, you're dumber than I thought."

"Kenly, I like what we have going on. Putting a title on things will complicate things and---"

I interjected his statement before he could finish, I was tired of hearing excuses after excuses. Some days, he told me that we didn't need a title because our bond was stronger than a title. Other times, he told me his love for me should be enough. The list of his excuses went on and on, but I know one thing, I'm sick of hearing it.

"I don't even know why I'm arguing with you. Nothing has changed from t day one, and it's my stupid ass fault. I thought in time you'd be ready for something serious. It's been some good times, but I'm done with this shit! Feel free to let yourself out while I shower alone." I had to fight back the tears that were forming in my eyes.

After all this time, this is what Jaylen and I have been reduced to, nothing but a friendship that never became a relationship. As much as it hurt me to end things, I knew in my heart he would never want the same things as me. I didn't deserve to keep being unhappy.

I stormed into the bathroom and locked the door. I prayed by the time I finished showering he had sense enough to leave my place and truly leave me alone for good this time. I've called it quits with Jay many times, but this time was different; I'm fed up. We all know from R. Kelly's famous song when a woman's fed up, there ain't nothin' you can do about it.

Thirty minutes later, I finished showering, put on a matching night set from PINK, and poured myself a huge glass of Chardonnay. I turned on some Keyshia Cole, singing my heart out to the chart-topping hit *"Trust and Believe"* as tears poured from my almond shaped brown eyes. I was going to fix myself another glass of wine when I thought there was no point in drinking alone. I gathered my belongings and locked my front door heading to Cherish's apartment. Cherish moved two floors down from me when she relocated to Greensboro. Times like this made me beyond grateful that she lived so close. I thought about calling Brittish over to console me too, but she's never been great at comforting others.

"Who is it banging on my door like they're the damn police? Ugh. I thought this was a quiet neighborhood," I could hear her saying as she approached the door. The door swung open, and her scrunched up facial expression turned into a look of concern as she took in the state of mind I was in. I broke down crying at her front door, almost dropping the wine I had in my left hand. She pulled me into her place, sitting me down on her Sofia Vergara gray couch, and held me for what felt like a century, letting me shed my hurt away.

When I finally stopped shaking and doing the ugly cry, she asked the awaiting question, "What happened, Kenly?"

"I broke things off with him. I don't need your judgements, or I told you so. I knew this situation wouldn't last forever, but I wish it could have ended differently. I gave him a year to get his shit together, a year of my life that I can't get back. Ugh, I should've cut his dick off." An evil smiled graced my face at the thought of hurting his manhood.

"First off, you can't harm him even if that's what he deserves. I know you're hurt, trust me, I know better than anybody else how you're feeling. Yes, you've lost a year of time, but you don't have to spend any more time crying or waiting on him. Kenly, we're going to be twenty-four soon. These are the years to be living our best lives, not sitting around crying over these trifling ass men." She hopped to fix me a fresh glass of wine and passed me a box of tissues.

"Touché, bitch. You've been living under a rock since your break up with Dame."

"That's very true but moving here opened my eyes to the life I should've been living all along. Let's put the past behind us and enjoy the rest of chapter twenty-three."

We clinked our glasses together. "Cheers to moving forward!" we exclaimed in unison.

Chapter 4

Two Weeks Later

Jared

I opened the double doors to Wells Fargo and took the elevator to the third floor. A young nigga finessed the second interview and landed a full-time job. I was looking good and feeling better. I wore a gray tailored suit accented with a yellow dress shirt, gray tie, and black dress shoes, nothing too fancy but impressive enough to show the world I was a man about his business. At twenty-six, my life was starting to come together. I came from a two-parent household, but watching my dad beat my mom's ass for most of my childhood had an influence on a nigga.

My mom and I had just gotten home from the grocery store, and the look on my dad's face created fear in my heart. His face would tell what kind of day it would be in the Daniel's household. My mom urged me to go to my room, like she always does when shit was going to hit the fan between the two of them.

"Tasha, you really like to see a nigga at his worst. Why would you wear that revealing ass outfit out of the house? Never mind, don't answer that. I know why you did it! Your ass is always trying to be seen!" my dad raged, pacing back and forth on the wooden tile.

"Babyyy, I didn't mean to defy you. It's ninety degrees outside, Ralph; it's too hot to be wearing long sleeves for Pete's sake," my mom said as she went to the kitchen to put the groceries up.

"You're going to learn one way or the other to respect me!"

Next thing I heard was WHAP! WHAP! WHAP!

"Ralph! Stop it! I promise I'll listen to you next time! Please stop it!" my momma pleaded as the true maniac inside of my dad was about to show up and show out.

Whenever my parents argued, I could hear them from my room, and I never came out of the room until he started hitting my mom. In a weird way, I hated to watch her get beat, but I needed to ensure he never took his abuse too far.

I heard the closet door open and close. I assumed he was punishing my mom by locking her in the closet for the night, which is a form of punishment he enjoyed the most after he got a few hits off.

"Noooo! Ralph, what are you doing with the bat!" my mom cried.

My ears perked up in an alarming manner. I watched from the guest bathroom with tears streaming from my childlike eyes as my father repeatedly hit my mom's body with a steel silver bat, he used for playing baseball. He hit her in the stomach a few times until I heard her ribs crack. I couldn't watch the horrid scene in front of me any longer.

I ran into my parents' room to call for help. For the first and only time in my life, I dialed 911. I was speaking so fast to the dispatcher that I was stuttering over my words.

I continued to hear the bat being swung in the air, my mom crying and pleading for my dad to stop until there was silence. I got nervous, not knowing if my mom had survived this time around. I peeked out of the bathroom to see the bloody bat on the floor. Moments later, I saw him crying and dropping to his knees. I rushed out of the bathroom in fear that something was seriously wrong with my mom since my dad *had started crying, which is something he's never done before, no matter how mad he got.*

The scene before me was gruesome. My mom laid lifeless on the wooden tile with blood splattered on the floor and cream-colored walls. Her caramel skin was replaced with purple and black bruises. My dad was shaking my mom begging her to wake up and promising that he'll never hit her again. I just stood there in a state of shock as more tears fell from my eyes, and the sound of the police sirens became louder and louder.

My momma was the sweetest person I knew, and she loved my father to death, literally. The night I called the police was the same night she was pronounced dead at ten-twenty-one p.m., forever changing the course of my life. My father was sentenced to twenty-five years in jail for assault with a deadly weapon and second-degree murder. I was sent to live with my maternal grandmother, better known as Pearl Simpson.

Years after my mom's death, I was twenty-one-years-old, dating this fine ass slim thick mixed breed named Khari. Khari was a good girl, but she had some ways about her that made a nigga rough her up a few times. Although I'm against a man putting his hands on a woman, when I get mad, I tend to blackout and forget this golden rule.

It was a typical Friday night, getting dressed to hang out with my homeboys from the hood. Khari was pissed I wasn't staying the night at her mom's house that tonight. I sprayed on some Ralph Lauren cologne and kissed Khari on her pretty pink Angelina Jolie lips. Out of nowhere, this bitch slapped me, accused me of cheating on her, and using my homeboys as a convenient excuse.

First off, she thought shit was sweet since she was bold enough to hit a nigga. Secondly, I've never cheated on her, which is why I was more than confused on where these accusations were stemming from.

She didn't give me time to explain before she started calling me all types of fuck niggas and saying I'm another trifling black man as she swung her arms at me. One of her fists connected to my left eye, and I blacked out.

I hadn't realized I had beaten her face in and was choking the life out of her until her mom rushed into the room pointing a gun at me saying, "Get your hands off my daughter, or I'm shooting."

To make a long story short, I was dragged off the premises in handcuffs, and Khari was wheeled into the ambulance on a stretcher. I never wanted to be like my father, and technically, in a sense, I wasn't an abuser; I just snapped when she kept hitting me. I was being charged with assault, battery, and a first-degree felony because I broke her nose and left significant markers around her neck and face. Although I told my truth and surprisingly, she co-signed my story after she realized those rumors of me cheating on her were just that, rumors, despite the truth being exposed, the jury and judge decided to give me a sixteen-month sentence, three years of probation, and anger management. I've always wondered why I had to do probation after jail time, but it was either do probation or have a longer stint in jail, so probation it was.

Here I am five years later, done with probation, working as a street pharmacist, and finally having my criminal record expunged. Selling some work was the only way to put money in my pockets as a convicted felon. I was tired of risking my life for a temporary come up which led to me looking for a legit job. Since my homeboy knew somebody who cleaned up criminal records, I was able to apply at a bank. I knew this salary gig wasn't going to be nothing like drug money, but after being in prison, I didn't plan on going back to do an even longer stint behind some drug shit. With my good looks, a new job, and freedom from the system, life was bound to go up from here.

I made it to the third floor where I checked in with Tori, the front desk assistant. The beautiful, talented, Hershey kiss named Ms. Wright came up front to retrieve me. Got damn, this woman was everything I needed in my life. In the words of J. Cole, "My girl got a diploma, she got wife written all over." She was educated, a little boujee, yet down to earth, sexy, but classy with it.

I caught a glimpse of her face before she turned her back to me. I noticed she wore minimal if any makeup with some red lipstick bringing attention to her plumped lips. I appreciated a natural woman. Girls nowadays look like clowns with all that makeup caked on and straight up ridiculous with long oversized lashes and thirty-inch weave. She wore a red flared mini skirt that stopped a few inches above her knee, a denim quarter length blouse tucked inside of her skirt accented with a red belt bow in the front encasing her waist with some nude Christian Louboutins. Just as my eyes traveled from her chocolate legs to her waist area, I noticed a gold David Yurman bracelet on her wrist. In her ears were some diamond gold studded earrings, and her jet-black hair swayed back and forth on her shoulders as she walked. From the looks of things, shawty had style and expensive taste. I didn't mind that though, I still had enough drug money stacked up to keep her laced in designer for a while. The way she strutted in front of me, made me want to know more about her.

"Thank you for being patient with us. The hiring process around here is tedious and quite frankly annoying. Here's the hiring packet that contains your salary, benefits, dates for training, and anything else that pertains to your new position."

"Out of all the things you listed, I didn't hear you mention your number as part of the deal. What's up with that?"

"I'm flattered, really I am. However, I don't mix business with pleasure."

"Technically, after today, our business is finished. You work at the corporate building, and I'll be working at a different location. So, unless you find me unattractive, I don't see what the problem is."

"Umm… it's just... I haven't dated in a while. I find you very attractive, handsome in fact, but..." She stopped talking and avoided all eye contact with me.

"There should be no buts. You know you're beautiful as hell, Cherish," I voiced, calling her by the first name on her work badge while paying her an overdue compliment at the same time. She tried not to blush as she chewed on the corner of her bottom lip, indicating she was nervous.

"I'm not trying to rush into anything, but a simple date won't hurt nobody. The way I see it, if I'm single, you're single, then it's only right we mix and mingle a little bit." I spoke with confidence, attempting to apply pressure to the situation.

She clasped her hands together sitting them on top of her desk, resting her chin on her knuckles as she stared at the wall, taking in everything I said. Her office became silence, to the point that you could just hear the clock ticking. I made a loud "Ahem" noise to clear my throat. "If you need some time—" She cut me off mid-sentence.

"Sure. Let me check my schedule, and we can set something up. I'll get my assistant to look up your number and call you some time tomorrow." Her pondering face had turned into a pearly smile.

I felt myself getting agitated with her response. Why did her assistant have to contact me instead of her calling me herself, but I figured getting her to agree to a something was good enough for now.

"Great. Well I look forward to hearing from you soon. I'll see myself out."

"Wait, I'll walk you out."

I had finally worn her pretty ass down to the point where she wanted me in her presence. We walked out of her office, passing the front desk, and hopped onto the elevator. The ride down to the first floor was smooth and quick. In the little time we had together, I questioned her about her favorite hobbies and restaurant. She loved painting, writing, and shopping, but I already figured the third hobby was a given from her fashion sense. I loved the way her face lit up when she talked about the things she enjoyed. Just as she was going to reveal her preference in restaurants, the elevator bell dinged, and the silver doors opened.

I stepped out knowing the conversation was going to end here, but to my surprise she strolled out behind me ready to talk some more. I could listen to her sweet angelic voice all day long.

"Red Lobster is my favorite. Those cheddar baked biscuits are a fat girl's dream." She laughed, putting her manicured hand on her right hip. "I'm also a fan of Lucky 32, Crafted the Art of a Taco, or Print Works Bistro. If you couldn't tell, I'm a foodie."

"I like a girl that can eat. Don't worry, sweetheart; after your assistant gets in touch with me, I'll be taking you somewhere nice." I brushed my hand against her face in a flirtatious way.

"Well... I've been thinking instead of having my assistant communicate with you, it'll be fine if we just exchange numbers."

This was music to my ears as the biggest kool-aid smile spread across my face. I pulled out my iPhone X, put in the passcode, and handed her my phone. Out of nowhere, some random dude that was a few inches taller than me approached us. "Don't tell me this fuck nigga is the reason you've been blowing me off!" he ranted in an angry tone throwing his hands up in the air. I dropped my head down feeling like some bullshit was brewing in the air. I should've known a drop-dead gorgeous lady like her had a crazy-ex in the background.

Aaron

I stopped by the bank to do a deposit before the weekend. It was the first of the month, meaning the bank was booming with people who got paid monthly. I was standing in line replying to some text messages from my brother when I heard a familiar voice. I looked up from my phone and saw her. There she was again looking like a delectable meal, but this time, she was getting too acquainted with another male. I felt like she was playing hide and seek with me, where she'd resurface, but disappear the minute I tell her I want her.

She's standing there engaging and chuckling with a nigga that shouldn't even be an option. From the tailored suit he was wearing, I could tell he had some money, could wine and dine her for a bit, but he wasn't fucking with me. I sounded like a jealous mad man, but I wasn't feeling how she turned me down to only give this guy the time of day. I was planning to watch this moment play out, then use it against her the next time she acted like she wasn't trying to be bothered. Clearly, she was down for other men to be occupying her free time.

The minute he handed over his phone and caressed her cheek, I saw red. I forgot I was in public and a professional business man. I completely dismissed the fact I was the next person in line, when I approached them.

"Don't tell me this fuck nigga is the reason you've been blowing me off."

Her little buddy displayed a look of confusion, while she paused from typing on his phone giving me a scowling look.

"OH, MY GOD! You're worse than a side chick, you just won't go away. Last time I checked, I'm single. Are you stalking me now? Why the hell are you at my job?" She fired off question after question and some random accusations.

"First off, I'm not stalking you. I came to the bank to do a deposit. Instead of interrogating me, just let me know if this guy is the reason you keep blowing me off?"

This chick really had the nerve to roll her eyes and kept putting the rest of her number in his phone, while ole' boy was cheesing from ear to ear. She was trying to embarrass me, but little did she know she was going to be the one who's embarrassed if she kept up with these antics.

I snatched the phone out of her hand and quickly deleted her number before I tossed it over to ole' boy. "If you know what's best for you, you'll leave her alone. All she likes to do is play childish games," I stated.

"I don't want any problems. I was under the impression that she was a free lady. Looks like you two have some unfinished business to handle. I'm out." He threw up both hands as if a policeman said freeze, indicating he didn't want any smoke with me. I was pleasantly surprised that getting him to back off was easy.

Although Cherish's entire demeanor from the crossed arms, to one eyebrow being raised, to her lips being twisted up, showed she was pissed, she'd be thanking me later for getting rid of him. She was out of his league anyways.

Ole' boy was almost to the exit door when I heard, "I'll get my assistant to call you about the date."

Instead of getting mad, I decided to play it cool knowing her assistant wouldn't be calling him. Some of the bank traffic took an interest in the heated moment we were having near the lobby. I smoothly stepped in front of her, grabbed her chin, crushing my lips against hers. Her plush pink lips felt like heaven against mine. She parted her lips just enough for me to slide my tongue inside to explore her mouth. I felt her moans vibrating against my lips.

"Shittt!" She declared as she put an end to our moment. She took a few steps back from me, placing both her hands over her lips as her pretty brown eyes looked away from me as if she was ashamed. There was an awkward silence between us, but the sound of typing on a computer and rapid communication between the bankers and customers could be faintly heard. I wiped off the residue of her red lipstick, thinking to myself I won her over.

My thoughts were cut short, when I heard, "I was feeling you, Cherish, but having a crazy ass ex you're still in love with is too much baggage for me."

She took off power walking in his direction. "Waittt, he's not my ex. Truthfully, we've never dated. I don't know why he kissed me. Ughhhh! Let me explain."

"No worries, shawty. It's all good," he responded, pushing the glass door open and disappearing into the crowded streets.

She turned around to face me, with her pointer finger in the air, creating a closer proximity between us. "You've got some nerve showing up to my job, creating a scene, canceling dates, and kissing me passionately. Leave me the fuck alone!"

"I'm sorry ole boy dipped out on you, but he was a lame anyways, I did you a favor." I cracked up laughing to lighten the mood.

"You know what, I'm going to call security. You might have control everywhere else, but I'm the head bitch in charge of this bank," she replied while taking a moment to flash her name tag in my face to prove a point.

"Chill, it's not necessary to call anybody. I'll see myself out. But my business does business at this bank, so don't look too surprised the next time we run into each other."

I headed for the glass doors, but I wouldn't be me if I didn't make an asshole comment. "It was good to know I can make you moan like that, but you don't have to worry, love; I'm done chasing you."

She parted her thick lips to go in on my ass. Like most women, they can't never let a nigga have the last word.

"Hold up, hold up—"

RRRRR! RRRRR! RRRR! A piercing sound like the purge and flashing light signaled the fire alarm was going insane rung, ultimately drowning out whatever she was about to say. I took this as my cue to bounce as everyone was running out of the bank in fear.

Cherish

"Another day, another dollar," was my favorite motto to recite when I wasn't in the mood to go to work. I hit the snooze alarm one too many times this morning, and now, I'm going to be late. Oh well I'm my own boss.

It's been a few days since the shit show went down at the bank, and my mind had been on overload ever since. I really did want to go out with Jared but being kissed by Aaron created conflicting feelings. Aaron is very cocky and kind of aggressive. Who kisses somebody to only say I'm done chasing you? The good angel on my left shoulder is telling me despite the kiss being everything, I needed to leave him alone. The devil on the other shoulder is saying, *damn, he's fine as fuck, date him, sis.* I needed a girl's night to clear my mind and shuffle through the pros and cons of dating again. I sped through several stoplights while driving down W Market Street, finally pulling up and parking my car in the parking deck across the street from the office.

I stepped out of the car, grabbing my purse, and changed from my gold sandals to my red bottom heels. I hated wearing heels while I was driving. I used the ride up to the third floor to put on my game face and get my attitude in check. Arriving late meant I would be getting off later or taking work home with me, and neither option was appealing to me. I'll probably skip my lunch break to catch up on my work…yeah, that sounds like a plan.

Of course, Tori was the first face that greeted me, but she seemed happier than normal. Hmm, I wonder what that's about. I treated Tori like she was one of my girlfriends instead of a front desk assistant. She made me feel welcomed here and became a listening ear for me to vent about work, relocating, and just voicing my feelings on life.

I made my presence known to the other people on my floor before I headed to my office space. I unlocked the door, got settled in for the day, and fixed my daily dose of coffee with French vanilla creamer and six sugars. I sat down to formulate an email in regards to the firm alarm being set off two days ago. Somebody's bad ass son pulled the alarm as a joke and created a mad house inside the bank. People were running around like chickens with their heads cut off. The fire marshals and the police pulled up too. If I was that little boy's momma, I would beat the brakes off his bad ass. Stunts like this are exactly why I don't want kids.

***

Knock. Knock. I told the individual on the other side to come in even though I knew it was nobody but Tori. Hardly anybody else came to my office unannounced. "Girl, why do you bother knocking? If it's just you, you're more than welcome to walk in anytime unless the door is locked."

"Sorry boss, I'm not used to having a laidback supervisor, but I was coming to ask you what happened downstairs yesterday? Word on the street is you went ham on a customer." Tori stood half way in my office holding to the door handle with one hand for stability. I don't know why she was refusing to come in and sit down.

I took a sip of my coffee and got comfortable in my office chair. I gave her the rundown of the chaotic scene between Aaron, Jared, and myself. I even told her about my previous run ins with Aaron, and she felt just as confused as I did by his behavior.

"That sounds terribe, but in happier news, I come bearing gifts. There were a dozen pink roses delivered for you." She sat the bouquet of flowers on my desk. I took a whiff of the flowery aroma as I fumbled for the inserted memo card.

The mini note card read, ***"It's been a few days. Call me. -Aaron."*** What type of games was he playing? One minute, he's like, 'I want you to be mine', then he's done chasing me, but now he wants me to call him?

"Who are the flowers from? Whoever sent them has good taste in sending gifts."

"Take a seat, Tori. I need some advice." I took a sip of my coffee and got comfortable in my office chair. I gave her the rundown of the chaotic scene between Aaron, Jared, and myself. She felt just as confused as I did by Aaron's behavior.

"Boss lady, you should date them both. It's 2018, enjoy life, live a little bit. Whoever the better man will win." Tori had an interesting perspective but going from dating nobody to dating two people seemed overwhelming. I thanked her for being a listening ear, deciding to put making a decision on hold for most of the morning.

I embraced the smell of the roses again while I took a thirty-minute lunch break to eat my homemade Caesar salad and check in with my momma. My momma was my confidant and therapist wrapped into one. She advised me to see what's popping with Jared. She felt like Aaron was doing the most and throwing temper tantrums like a child, and she had a point. It was flattering to have two fine ass men checking for me, but I needed more than physical attraction. Anybody could fuck me good, but to love me correctly was a challenging task most men weren't cut out to do.

I stopped overthinking and pressed the blue call button under his name. The phone rung twice. "Hello Aaron, it's Cherish. I got your little gift, really cute."

"Good afternoon, love. I wasn't expecting to hear from you so soon."

"Yeah, I got your message, and today is your lucky day. The reason I'm calling is to tell you I'm willing to go on a date or whatever you want to decide to plan for us. I'm down."

"I finally wore your pretty ass down. Let's get together tomorrow night at my place, I want to cook for you. Be ready by seven, I'll send my driver to pick you up."

Impressive, he has a driver. I was far from broke, but I'm green to the lifestyle of being chauffeured around. There's a first time for everything. "Um... that's cool, I guess. I'll send you my address. You better make this night worth my wild, Mr. Ross."

"I aim to please, and I'd never disappoint you."

I couldn't handle giving two people my undivided attention, so I had to pick one, and naturally I chose him. Jared was cool, but Aaron took the cake; I saw something in him. Yeah, potential can be a hit or miss, but Aaron's sweet gesture and continuous efforts won me over.

Chapter 5

Something New

Cherish

"Brittish, I think this outfit is too sexy for tonight."

"You look amazing, babe, Aaron's gonna love it," Brittish reassured me.

I ended our Facetime call, checking myself out in the mirror one more time. The red bodycon halter top dress hugged my curves in all the right places, with a pair of gold Jimmy Choo sandals. My hair was bone straight with a part down the middle to showcase my beauty. Maybe Brittish was right; I looked sultry and not too sexy.

It was nearing seven p.m. when I heard a knock at my front door. I figured it must've been Aaron's driver, so I didn't bother looking through the peep hole. I was pleasantly surprised, to come face to face with a tall black man named Black. He helped me down the stairs into a cream-colored Escalade with leather tan seats on the inside.

"Buckle up, Ms. Wright. We'll be to Mr. Ross' condo shortly."

On the way to his place, I shared my location with Brittish in case something happened to me. I was going to tell Kenly, but I knew she'd raise my anxiety with a million and one questions.

The escalade came to a halt when Black typed in a code to get us past the silver gate. Shortly after, Black guided me to his front door on the fourth floor, using his key to let me in. When I walked in, the smell of apple cinnamon and food filled my nostrils.

Aaron met me in the foyer while Black made himself ghost for the rest of the evening.

"Good evening, pretty lady. It's good to see you again after asking you out numerous times," he expressed. He went in for a hug and placed a kiss on my cheek.

"Don't start, it's not too late for me to walk out the door just as quick as I walked in."

"Alright, my bad, I worked too hard to let you leave me again. Don't be shy, make yourself at home. I'm almost done with dinner."

I sat my gold clutch on the counter and started looking around his living room. I was mesmerized by a big glass window showcasing the city view of downtown. I gazed at a family portrait where everybody was wearing all white looking like the royal family. He continued to impress me with his lavish lifestyle.

"You must have hired an interior decorator or had your momma decorate the place, it's too decked out for you to be a man."

"What's that supposed to mean? Men can be stylish too. It's only right my condo reflects the lifestyle I'm living.

I continued to tour his place, taking in the essence of his customized bachelor pad. I busied myself with looking through his photo albums while I sat on the couch, until it was time take a seat at the dining room table. I couldn't wait to see the entrée he chose to cook. He prepared lemon garlic salmon, rice, and steamed vegetables; the food almost looked too good to eat. He also popped open a bottle of red wine pouring me a glass.

I sliced off a piece of salmon with a spoon full of rice instantly saying, "Umm, this is good! Your ass can really cook."

"Thank you. I do my thing in the kitchen every now and then," he said confidently. I rolled my eyes wondering why I complimented his conceded ass. I went back to indulge the rest of my meal.

"So, outside of work, enlighten me on your likes, hobbies, dislikes. Take your time and tell me more about Cherish Wright." I chewed on my bottom lip trying to think of where I should start with my life story. It's been too long since I played the get to know you game.

His simple statement led to a deep conversation about our careers, family, and marriage, pretty much the rundown of everything you'd want to know about somebody. We both loved our families, valued having a career, and envisioned getting married one day. However, the nature of the conversation shifted when the topic of kids was on the table. He wanted a couple of legacies to carry on the Ross name, but I felt borderline against having kids. I mean, they're cute and everything, but giving life and being held responsible for another human being made me feel uneasy.

He left the kitchen a mess grabbing my hand and walking me over to the balcony behind the gorgeous glass window. I placed my hands on the silver bar handle gazing into the dark sky.

"It's beautiful and so peaceful out here. I wish we could stay in this moment forever." The downtown city view was breathtaking, and my hopeless romantic ass couldn't help getting sentimental. stood behind me for a minute gripping my waist. Out of nowhere he started humming and singing acapella, *"You Got it Bad"* by Usher.

"Tell her, I'm your man, you're my girl,

I'm gonna tell it to the whole wide world."

I forgot to mention besides pretty eyes, a man that could sing would send a wet wave to my panties. I turned around facing his chest looking up to his face. He leaned down kissing me slowly, and unlike last time, I wanted this kiss. I cupped my hands around his face as I meshed my tongue with his. Tonight has been nothing short of amazing.

Brittish

It's going on eight o'clock that night, and I was stuck in the lab running test on these fluids. I'm running a DNA test for the third time because the prior results were inconsistent. I'm a laboratory technician at Lab Corps. Patients come in to get their cheeks swabbed, and two teams are responsible for getting the DNA results. Most of the time, both teams get the same results, and the director can send out a letter to the client letting them know the outcome. However, we got different results, and I volunteered to handle my teams' part before I left from work this evening.

I was beyond exhausted. Doing a nine-hour shift had taken its toll on me, but I love my career, nonetheless. Almost an hour later, the DNA results popped up on the screen, reading probability of paternity: 99.9%. I threw my hands up in the air thanking God another black child wouldn't grow up not knowing who their father is. I emailed the results to my director, quickly shut the computer system down, and locked up the office. The security guard watched me walk to my car before he returned to his post.

I turned on the "For the Culture" radio on Apple music and hopped on to I-40, heading to see my king. Speaking of him, I saw he was calling me as my music was cut off through the Bluetooth system.

I hit the answer button. "Hey babe, are you off work yet?" He wondered with the anticipation of me saying yes.

"You know I'm on my way over there. I just left from the office. I'll see you in few. You must be fiending for some, Brittish," I mentioned playfully. After a long day like this, I looked forward to seeing my man.

"Brittish, I'm always fiending for my fiancé. Drive safe and meet me in the shower when you get here."

I tapped the gas pedal harder to increase my speed, as thoughts of what tonight holds for Grant and me flooded my mind. Grant was my mother fuckin' baby, and everybody in the city knew this. Unlike Cherish and Kenly, no shade intended, I found a quality man that didn't have me looking stupid nor was he running the streets.

I met him at a cookout my job hosted for new hires once I moved back to Greensboro. He was invited to the party by one of the supervisors from Lab Corps. Grant was dark chocolate gentlemen that stood at six-foot-one. He had dreads that hung down his back and a Balbo beard. He's the total opposite of me which complimented me in many ways. I'm a red bone with burgundy colored hair and dark brown freckles. I didn't have a big booty, but it was enough to grip and hold on too. A mixture of chocolate and vanilla always took the cake.

During the party, my boss introduced the two of us, and it's been history ever since. We were together for a little over eight months, when he decided to propose on Valentine's day. Although I'm twenty-four, some people disapproved of the engagement, but I happily said "yes" anyways. In a couple of months, I was going to be Mrs. Grant Jamal Taylor.

I pushed past the gate, parked my car, and walked inside his condo. I opened the front door and followed the rose petals that led to his bedroom. I heard the shower running and *"When We"* remix by Tank playing over the speaker as I stripped out of my work attire.

I walked in the bathroom noticing he had started showering without me. I didn't mind though, since I had to wrap up my hair. I went through too much at the Dominican salon this morning to get my hair wet.

"Who came to make sweet love? Not me,

Who came to kiss and hug? Not me,

Who came to beat it up? Rocky."

I slid the shower door open and stepped inside. Grant grabbed my ass, while kissing me passionately. The hot water cascaded down my skin as a soft moan escaped my lips. Grant started placing kisses on my neck, making his dick rock up. As much as I wanted to share this moment with him, I told him, "Babe, did you forget I got slayed earlier today?" Grant let out a huff. I knew he was mad I killed the moment, but he also knew I didn't play about my hair. I didn't get my scalp torched by a blow dryer for no reason.

"Let's speed this shower up. I'm ready to dive into something tight and wet," he stated, grabbing the Dove shea butter body wash. Two more songs had finished playing by the time we finished showering and drying off.

Grant went to put some boxers on, while I slipped on my silk robe from Victoria Secret. I pulled open the cabinet door, in search of my Johnson's baby oil. I prefer to oil my smooth skin instead of using lotion.

I walked into the bedroom, plopping down on the edge of the king size bed to start oiling down my legs. I was about to handle my feet next, when Grant sat down beside me, taking the bottle from me, and motioned for me to put my feet in his lap. He poured some oil in his hands and started massaging my right foot. I swear this man was too good to me. He knew I over worked myself today meaning my feet were killing me. He knew his lady liked the back of his hand.

We engaged in some small talk about each other's day. It was nice to catch up since I only got to talk to him briefly on my lunch break.

He hit my thigh. "Take your robe off and lay down on your stomach." I obliged his request.

He straddled his legs over my lower half as he poured more oil onto my back. If I didn't know any better, I would've thought he was a professional masseuse from the way he was rubbing away the tension in my shoulders. I was damn near sleep when I felt him dragging me to the edge of the bed. I should've known I wasn't going to sleep that easily, but I still decided to lay there pretending like I was snoozing.

I felt my legs being spread apart slightly, then a delicate kiss was placed on my pussy from the back before he went in for the kill. He feasted on my pussy like it was southern cuisine. My desire to go to sleep quickly resided. He switched from attacking my love box with his tongue to using his thumb to play with my clit as he did slow licks up and down my slit. I could feel myself getting wetter and wetter with each lick. "Shitttt…Grant, don't stop, I'm about to cummmm." Not even a minute later, I released a powerful orgasm, and he gladly soaked up all my juices as if his life depended on it.

At this point, I was ready for some dick. I started to turn around and lay down on my back when Grant instructed me to stay face down with my ass tooted up. I followed his command, bracing myself to take every inch of his pipe from the back.

"Brittish, I hope you're ready to take our relationship to the next level."

His statement caught me off guard, peaking my interest. We had already taken our relationship to the next level by getting engaged, maybe he meant after we get married things would be official. After I get dicked down, I plan to ask more questions about his weird comment.

He grabbed both ass cheeks spreading them apart. Instead of feeling his dick entering me, I felt a wet sensation, realizing his tongue was sliding up and down the crack of my ass. I was stunned to say the least. "OH, MY GOD! Grant, what are you doing?" I asked, reaching my hand back in an attempt push his head away.

"Just let me do this, babe. I promise you're going to enjoy it."

He continued to shove his face in my booty, putting his tongue in my asshole. I've never had my ass eaten before, but I must admit the shit felt amazing. He started finger fucking my pussy as he kept one steady hand on my ass cheek continuing to go to work on my ass. This shit here was on another level, for real. I felt that feeling creeping up in my stomach again as I yelled out, "I'm cumming again, fuck!"

"Get your nut off, boo," he spoke into my tunnel of love, giving me permission to release all over his blemish free face.

Those two orgasms took a lot out of me, but I knew Grant had to get his relief too. He flipped me over, putting my legs up on his shoulder guiding his dick inside of me. He started off with slow deep strokes making sure I felt all of him. He leaned down for a kiss, and I started sucking on his tongue and bottom lip. I could taste my lady parts on his lips, savoring the flavor. Not only does my honey pot taste fye, so does my ass.

"Damn, Brittish, this pussy is the truth." He sped up his stroke game and started drilling his dick inside me at full speed.

I was in a state of euphoria to the point that I was calling out his government name, "Grant Jamal Taylor…. I love youuu."

Grant started grunting and making that sex face that let me know he was about to cum. Moments later, we were cumming together. Grant kissed me passionately and confirmed how much he loved me too.

I can always count on my babe to knock it out of the park. Grant grabbed a warm rag to clean me up before he hopped back in the shower. My body was spent. I drifted off to sleep shortly after.

✳✳✳

"Sis, are you up? I've been itching to tell somebody about tonight," Cherish voiced on the other end of the line, while I attempted to wipe the crust out of my eyes.

"I was sleeping, boo. Grant dicked me down so good, girl, I was knocked out like a sleeping baby." I chuckled, flashing back to getting my ass ate for the first time. I hope he planned to surprise me like that again. If I didn't know it before, I knew now. I had his heart, body, and mind on lockdown.

I eased out of the bed being careful not to wake up Grant, feeling around the dark room for my robe and fuzzy slippers. "What time is it? You couldn't wait until tomorrow to fill me in on your love life?" I babbled question after question, tying my silk robe closed as I headed down the stairs quietly, settling down on the couch.

"Geez Brittish, too many damn questions at once. It's twelve-thirty a.m.; you're acting like you can't spare ten minutes of sleep. Plus, this news is too hot to wait until tomorrow," she retorted into the phone with an attitude. Cherish despised being asked a series of questions, yet she often did the same madness to other people. I rolled my eyes letting this attitude of hers become an afterthought.

"You got twenty minutes, spill the tea."

Her voice became high pitched, no longer hiding her excitement. "As you already know, his assistant named Black came to scoop me up and drove me to his condo. Initially, I felt skeptical about driving Miss Daisy, hence the reason I shared my location with you. Black turned out to be chill, nonchalant, and escorted me to Aaron's place. His condo was nice as fuck, expensive furniture, top of the line appliances, and the apple cinnamon aroma was everything."

As I listened to her, I was taken by surprise because most men don't believe in fixing up their apartments. It's tacky when a man only cares about having a futon and that damn Xbox instead of spicing up the place. No female wants to sit on a funky ass futon that's not even considered a real couch.

"I bet you was damn near weak when you smelled your favorite scent, apple cinnamon."

"Bitchhh...my nose thought I was in cinnamon heaven for the night." She giggled into the receiver.

"Sis, the night got better. He can cook like a chef on Chopped. The taste of salmon with rice was a blessing with a glass of Moscato."

"Wait a minute, girl. A black man that has his own, can cook, and quality taste in wine is a reason to start shouting. You've almost got you a similar version of Grant."

"Can I finish my moment before you talk about Grant? Everybody knows he treats you like queen, but like I was saying, he took me outside on the balcony giving me an exquisite view of downtown at night. It was breathtaking, and he had me weak in the knees when he started singing. I know this may sound crazy and be too soon to say this, but I feel comfortable in his presence as if I've known him for a while," Cherish vocalized.

I was over the moon ecstatic to hear this type of news from her. Cherish loved hard and gave her all in relationships and friendships. After everything that happened with Dame, she became closed off to loving romantically again. I know she's not totally over him, but the mere fact that she finally stepped away from the norm and went on a date spoke volumes. I silently sent up a prayer to God for my best friend. She deserved happiness and the love she's constantly giving to others.

"I'm happy for you, sis! He sounds like a good guy... I'm not trying to ruin the mood, but I've always been team Dame. I just want you to know if things progress between you two, I'll accept him with open arms."

"Thanks, best friend. Everybody was rooting for Dame and me, but that ship has sailed. I'm emotionally and mentally ready to let the past remain the past. I was just telling Kenly two weeks ago how it's time for us to start living our best life." I could tell in her voice she was being serious this time.

"I second that motto, Cee!"

Cherish and I stayed on the phone for half an hour discussing our favorite ratchet reality shows from *Love and Hip Hop: Atlanta* to *The Real Housewives of Atlanta.* The rumor mill swears reality shows are scripted, but I couldn't get enough of the ratchetness. The fact that people will expose their marital problems and friendships for a check is the definition of ratchet.

The sound of my stomach rumbling caused me to look in the direction of the clock ticking, seeing it was two in the morning. It wasn't too late to fix myself a big bowl of ice cream. I strolled into the kitchen, deciding to eat straight from the Haagen-Dazs strawberry carton. I greedily shoved a spoonful into my mouth, licking the spoon and everything.

"Sis, I'm going to call it a night. Thanks again for listening and being supportive."

"Of course, girl, I wouldn't be a real friend if I left you hanging, and don't forget about my bridal appointment next week. "

"No worries. The appointment has been saved in my phone and work schedule for weeks now. Also, can you keep the news about Aaron between us for now?I plan to tell Kenly about him soon, but right now, she's recovering from the Jaylen, and I don't want to rub my happiness in her face. I hope you understand."

"Okay, boo. Your secret is safe with me, goodnight." I closed my eyes praying to God I could keep another secret. I already felt guilty for holding in one gut wrenching secret.

"I guess I didn't put in enough work tonight if you're out of the bed at this hour," Grant stated.

He startled the shit of me, putting my inner thoughts on hold. I dropped the sterling silver spoon, putting my hand over my racing heart.

I turned around with a resting bitch facial expression, "Didn't your momma ever tell you not to sneak up on black people?"

"Yeah, Moms raised me right, but did you forget that I live here? More importantly, why are you up at one-thirty in the morning eating ice cream and talking to yourself?" He walked over to me looking sexy as fuck, holding his arms around me. I could feel him breathing on my neck when he inquired why I was wide awake.

I picked up the spoon to scoop up some ice cream, allowing it to melt in my mouth as an awkward silence filled the room. Grant tightened the grip he had on my waist, letting me know he was still waiting for an answer.

I closed the ice cream carton, inhaling some air and letting out a deep sigh. "Babe, the dick and spit game were mind blowing. Trust me, I was knocked the hell out until Cherish called me. She wanted to spill some tea about her date night."

"Woah. Pause. Wait. Did you say Cherish went on a date? Cherish, the one that's been on a man-cation for too long? The one that swore all niggas ain't shit including the niggas she's never fucked with?"

I rolled my eyes. "Yes, that Cherish, fool!" I turned around quickly to hit him on the chest which caused the both of us to start cracking up laughing.

"Damn boo, no wonder you look stressed. Cherish going on a date is a big fucking deal. Let me guess though, he's a fuckboy?"

"Actually no... he's a great guy," I responded slowly. "She's planning to go out with him again on Sunday."

"So, why are you stressed? I'm lost. Y'all have been trying to get her to date somebody for quite some time. Now, she's taking the advice, and you're worried?" he questioned me, raising his eyebrows giving me a puzzled look.

"The problem is I'm tired of holding onto this secret about Dame. Every time I want to tell her, the timing isn't right. Before, she was too heartbroken. Now, she's about to ride off into the sunset with Aaron. When she finds out the truth, she'll never forgive me."

Cherish was the type of person that never let shit go. Once you're on her shit list, nobody but God could change how she felt about you. As her best friend, I should be able to tell her anything, and normally, I would, but this secret is different.

"Listen. The truth may hurt, but it's better than continuing to lie. She's been your homegirl for five years now. I don't believe she'll throw your friendship away. She might stop fucking with you for a while, but y'all will get back cool at some point."

I marinated on Grant's perspective of the situation, praying to the highest God that he was right. I believed in praying to God for everything. I'm a sinner who's probably going to sin again, but even I know God was the one to go to for all my problems. I never want to fall out with a friend over a nigga, especially a nigga that's not even my nigga.

I ran my lime green stiletto nails across his broad chest looking into his eyes. "Thanks, babe."

He gripped my ass cheeks, snaking his head down to meet my awaiting lips. My tongue did a dance with his as I wrapped my arms around his neck. I could feel his manhood raising against my stomach.

"You already know what time it is, beautiful." He was referring to the beat down my pussy was going to endure once more.

I bat my mink lashes, shaking my head up and down in agreement. He picked me up, placing me on the marble countertop, and untied my robe revealing my naked body. He stared at me in awe. "Don't let nobody tell you you're not perfect." Hearing those words made my juices ooze onto the counter. I loved that Grant was romantic and reminded me daily how much he loved and appreciated me, but in this moment, I wanted him to fuck me good and long. He could save the sentimental shit for tomorrow.

I pulled him closer to me, placing kisses on his bare chest as I pulled his out manhood through the opening of his Polo boxers. I slid down closer to the edge, feeling him enter my middle seconds later.

I wrapped my legs tightly around his waist enjoying the pleasure of him pounding in and out of my love box.

Chapter 6

It's A Man's World

Jared

"Ayo Malik, hand me the weigh scale," I hollered at my homeboy while I was breaking down some loud into a grape swisher, pearling that shit to perfection. I took a long hit from the blunt allowing my mental to be at ease. After a couple more pulls I passed the blunt to Malik. Malik is my childhood homie that's been there through my momma's death and held me down during my jail sentence. He's helped me stay up even when life had counted me out.

I pulled a brick of cocaine out of my black bag, fumbling in the top drawer of desk I was sitting at searching for a knife. I set up the area with the scale, knife, and plastic baggies preparing to break down two bricks. I'm on a mission to prepare and sell this product quickly. The sooner I push this work the sooner I can end this temporary job.

He put the scale on the table, "I've been meaning to tell you congrats on getting the job. I told you Phoenix would come through on the background check." Phoenix is a professional hacker that swiped my record clean.

"I can't believe you're going to give up this lifestyle so soon. Your trading in the fast cash and bad bitches for a 9 to 5," he stated. He started helping me bag up the coke after I weighed it.

"This lifestyle has it's perks but the thought of going back to prison is a no go. We both know I never wanted to be a dope dealer but with my record the chances of getting a legit job was slim to none."

I've been out on probation for three months. After several failed attempts to secure a job, I took Malik's offer to be a member of his team. Malik been a dealer for a few years, working under a kingpin named Roman. The plan was to work the block selling some weed until the felony charge was removed from my record. I started out at the bottom like any new member, but a few weeks ago, prior to my job interview, I got promoted to selling coke.

Moving up from weed to coke was the blessing I needed. Coke was guaranteed money that upgraded my wardrobe, purchased my 2018 Dodge Charger, and allow me to pay up on the rent for a year once I found an apartment. I had to live with my grandma until I wrapped up probation. After I sell these two bricks for $50k I was planning to stack back most of the money in my safe and open a bank account.

A lot of dope dealers don't associate with banks, but I envision my future as a businessman. Nobody would take me seriously if I didn't have an account and a legal way of making income, hence my purpose in working a 9 to 5. Yes, I'm a convicted felon but I'm far from dumb. I've always had dreams of having my own and being able to say I've made my momma and grandma proud; fuck my sperm donor.

Let me be clear, the street life is dangerous, but I wasn't a pussy ass nigga. I just didn't want to spend my life looking over my shoulder or continuing to make purchases in my grandma's name because I didn't technically have a real job. Plus, I want a family one day which further motivated me to get out of the game.

Thanks to Roman and Phoenix my wishes were coming true sooner than I thought they would. Being a bank teller was a huge pay cut from my current revenue, but it'll take care of my needs until I figure out what type of business I wanted to open or invest in.

"Malik, we were raised in the projects, Smith Homes to be exact. The odds were never in our favor, so the mere fact that I'm out of jail and have some racks stashed away is good enough for me." The problem in the drug world is people start making big money and getting greedy to the point that killing their boss or losing family members becomes an afterthought.

"I respect your opinion, bro. Everybody isn't cut out to be a dope dealer. This lifestyle requires late nights and keeping your bitches in line. However, the lavish cars and 2 million dollars I've saved up between bank accounts and safes makes living this life worth it." Malik walked over to the entrance of the back room, closing the door tightly to give us some privacy. The traffic in the trap house was booming. All the dealers under Roman's team were racking up on products for the week. A shipment of coke, molly, weed, and opiates came in every Friday, allowing the us to re-up on Sundays. It felt good to know after these two bricks are sold, I'm done with this shit.

Malik resumed his role of helping me. "I haven't shared this with anybody yet, but Roman wants me to take over. He's getting older and he's ready to get out of the game. Within the next year he's passing the position along to me, making me the next kingpin," he spoke smoothly, rubbing he's hands together like birdman.

Wow, Malik was going to be that nigga. I figured one day he'd grow tired of this lifestyle, but I thought wrong. "Congrats... I guess." I replied dryly, finishing up cutting and weighing my last brick.

Silence filled the air until somebody knocked on the door. "Jared. Malik. Are y'all almost done back here? I could use some help getting this order together for a frat party that's going down near UNCG." Lennox asked.

White college kids were the perfect match for a dope dealer. They were rich brats that used drugs to cope with college and trying to live up to their family standards. I tucked away the baggies in my black bag, getting up from the desk, and throwing the bag over my shoulder. Rule number two is never leave our products unattended and rule number one is always get the money first.

We took a stroll down the noisy hallway until we reached the kitchen area. Before us was a long rectangular table that was supposed to be for dining purposes. There was 20 ounces of weed, various opiates, and three bricks of coke." Damn, how many motherfuckers attending this party?" I asked Lennox, taking in the number of narcotics presented before me. I've seen hella drugs, shit I'm a drug dealer but these white kids were trying to burn their brains out in one night.

"Man, I don't ask about the numbers. I just supply the requested products. I think the young dude that's hosting the party mentioned that midterms were going down this week. They plan to get lifted like never before from all the stress they're facing.

I never dreamed of going to college and from the way Lennox was talking I'm glad I didn't go. Between the course load, family drama, and curveballs that life throws you would make anybody start doing drugs.

I personally only rock with weed and occasionally I pop some molly if I'm on the edge about something. If my memory serves me correctly, the last time I popped one was a few days ago when ole' buddy went ham at the bank. Normally I would have laid his bitch ass out but thanks to anger management and probation I decided to keep my hands to myself. How was I supposed to know she was his girl? I should've known she was too fine to be single.

Until I meet a quality lady that understands my life story and future endeavors, I was cool with being single. Outside of wetting up my dick from time to time, females were useless to me. The last bitch I fucked with damn near ruined my life, recalling the faint memories of Khari.

Lennox connected his phone to the blue tooth system, increasing the noise volume within the house. Narcos by Migos set the vibe for the moment as we each picked a product, a scale, and zip lock bags to formulate this order.

Aaron

"Wade successfully shot another three pointer! Miami Heat and Charlotte Hornets are tied with a score of 78-78!" the male announcer blared through the television. A big kool-aid smile graced my face as the possibility of winning a bet with my father became my reality.

"Damn Pops. I told you Wade was nasty on the court. You should've picked a better team." I bragged on Wade some more, grabbing my corona from the coffee table, taking a swig.

"Son, we still have overtime. That's more than enough time to win the bet. I'll be damned if I'm losing $100 over an NBA 2k game. Prepare for destruction Ace," my pops spoke with confidence, calling me by my nickname.

My brother Romelo Ross was named after my father and I was named after my grandfather, Aaron Ross. I know it's weird, but my family wanted the Ross name to be carried out to the fullest. Even though my brother and I were both technically juniors, he took on the nickname as Junior and everybody called me Ace to keep the confusion at a minimum.

My dad was the coolest laid-back man I knew. He's the reason I'm the man that I am today. He got his CDL straight out of high school, attending North Carolina Agricultural and State University (NCAT) for a degree in business. Following college, he married his high school sweetheart who's my beautiful mother, Tonya. He started Ross Trucking and Moving company before he turned 30 and retired at 55 years old. My older brother and I followed in his footsteps, getting a business degree and taking over the Ross family legacy. In my eyes my dad was that nigga. If I could live up to be half the man that he was, I'd be proud of myself.

The clock for the five minutes of overtime started with my team getting the ball during tip off. My dad talked shit when he made some successful shots, but he was no match for me when I hit a three pointer as the final buzzer went off.

"Hell, yeah Wade that's what the fuck I'm talking about! Run me my money ole' man!" I shouted jumping up from the couch. The ending score was 95-92.

"Why are you yelling in my house? Better yet, why are you cussing?" my momma questioned, entering the living room. I kissed her on the cheek, "My apologies mom, I didn't hear you come in."

"Just because your dad plays that cursing and carrying on business, doesn't mean I'm here for it." She took off towards the kitchen to prepare Sunday dinner.

My mom was the opposite of my pops. She believed in having class and respecting your elders. Outside of being slightly boujee, my momma was a phenomenal woman. She didn't look a day over 52. She stayed in the gym, maintained her wifely duties, and teaching English online. My dad wanted her to quit working when he retired, but she was adamant about teaching for a few more years.

"Son are you staying for dinner or do you have plans with one of your little hoes?" she yelled into the next room. My dad and I shook our heads knowing my mother was getting ready to go on another rant. She strongly disapproved of how I dealt with women. "I'll be glad when you get yourself together and bring home my future daughter-in law. It's ashamed that your brother has settled down and you're still playing...."

"Blah blah blah" were my thoughts as I attempted to tune my mother out.

My dad searched his wallet for a hundred-dollar bill while I finished my corona. I gloated when I took the money from my pops and walked into the kitchen to grab my car keys.

"Ace are you listening to me?" she asked while cutting some fresh vegs on a red cutting board.

"Yes, that boy hears you Tonya. I'm sure the whole neighborhood can hear you getting winded up," my dad chimed in on my behalf.

I decided to put my mother out of her misery and tell her about Cherish, hoping she'd get off my case for a little bit. "To answer your question mom, I'm going on a date but not with no little hoe. Her name is Cherish. She's a chocolate beauty who's going to make an honest man out of me. She's a good girl with the purest heart I've ever seen." I'm sure my face was lighting up as I spoke highly of her.

"Umph...I'm speechless." That's a first that Tonya Ross didn't have anything to say.

"It's good to know all of my nagging finally worked. I hope she can put up with you long enough for us to meet her.

"In due time I'll bring her around the family, but for now I'll see you good people later." I dapped my father up and hugged my momma before I headed out.

***

"Oh, my goodness, this buffalo chicken wrap is bomb," Cherish uttered in-between chewing her food. Shout out to Black for getting this picnic basket together. I swung by my place to get the basket and blanket before I picked Cherish up. My boy made the wraps, a fruit salad, chocolate chip cookies, and two bottles of Simply Lemonade. I made a mental note to give him a bonus check.

We chilled on the royal blue picnic blanket enjoying the food and each other's company. I kept staring at her, taking in her chocolate beauty. "Can you stop staring at me? Your making me nervous." Her dimple resurfaced indicating she was blushing.

"Sorry babe. Your beauty has me star struck. Let me take a picture of you for the gram." I snapped a few shots of her smiling. She wore a quarter sleeve denim romper accessed with gold diamond studded gladiator sandals that laced up around her calve muscle. Her hair was in a messy bun showing off her chocolate facial features and golden pearl earrings. I don't know too much about makeup but the pink and blue ombre eyeshadow and glitter surrounding her cheeks made her skin glow. I selected two of my favorite pictures, uploading it to IG with the caption saying *"Thinkin bout wifing her" and "It's her world I'm just happy to be living in it"*. I knew this post was going to bring some of my old hoes back to life, but I wanted to show off what was mine or should I say what was soon to be mine.

"Boy bye! Don't get your female followers worked up over a photo. You've messed with plenty of baddies before, but somehow your starstruck over me. Tuh, I've told you about trying to sweet talk me. It doesn't work on me."

"How many times do I have to tell you that your nothing like those other females. I swear I've been all about you since I saw you at the bank."

"Aaron, this is our second date and it's only been two weeks since the bank encounter. It's going to take more than two weeks before I feel secure. You're use to girls doing things at your pace and hanging on to your every word but I'm not that chick," she stated seriously.

Damn she read me like a book. I always convinced females to do things my way but Cherish wasn't having it. I liked her, could even see myself dating her exclusively but I wasn't used to a female calling me out on my shit.

The birds were chirping, and a plethora of people were walking through Bicentennial Gardens on a Sunday afternoon. I moved the paper plates and basket out of my way, getting closer to her.

"I know you're nothing like the type of woman I'm used to seeing. Let's clean up our mess and take a stroll around the gardens?"

She crossed her arms like she wasn't planning to move anytime soon. I was going to break her from this defiant attitude. I grabbed her face with my left hand, turning her face towards me. We had a stare off leading to me kissing her lips. Surprisingly she kissed me back slipping her tongue in my mouth intensifying the moment. I don't know what came over her, but she transitioned from sitting beside me to straddling my waist. I bit her bottom lip, keeping my hands in the safe zone not gripping her ass like I wanted too. She grasped a fist full of my red Ralph Lauren polo, throwing her arm over my shoulder. The thought of giving her the business was becoming irresistible, my hands had a mind of their own as they glazed her buns.

"Wait! No! I'm sorry!" She declared, ending the kiss and letting go of my shirt. Innocent bystanders stared at us in disgust making this situation more awkward by the second.

"This is too much way too soon. I don't know what's got into me." She removed my hands, hopped off my lap, and sat with her legs crisscrossed holding her head down like she was embarrassed of her behavior. She has the tendency to feel ashamed for wanting me. I know her ex did a number on her, but she didn't have to act like a baby every time our kisses got carried away.

Whether it was now or later, the plan all along was to feel her insides, but I wasn't going to push her to do something she clearly wasn't ready to do.

"Come here Cherish," I draped my arm around her. "There's no need to be sorry, we both got caught up in the moment. I wouldn't encourage you to do anything that you didn't want to do."

"Thanks. Despite what just happened, I'm not opening the cookie jar no time soon. I hope you understand and respect that."

"I can get with that Chocolate," causing her to smile.

"It's funny when you call me Chocolate because you're not too light bright yourself."

"True point, but I'm still going to call you Chocolate from time to time. Let's clean up and go for a walk for real this time."

I threw away the trash and packed up the remains of whatever else was left, while Cherish folded up the blanket. I hit the trunk button on my key ring, placing everything back there. The sun was beaming, the rust and yellow leaves hung from the trees, and the smell of flowers scented the atmosphere. It was warm for it to be October. North Carolina weather be on some other shit. I reached out for her hand as we strolled through Bicentennial Gardens.

Dame

"Cheers to the beginning of another successful basketball season. Bottoms up gentlemen!" one of my team players whispered in my ear, translating everything Coach Russo announced from Italian to English. The team and I threw back the first of many shots on this Tuesday night.

One of the cons of being an international baller is not fully understanding my coach, meaning I had to depend on the dual language player to translate for me. My second year in the league erupted with a bang by my team consecutively winning its third game.

Coach Russo was letting lose tonight. He's brought out an entire floor at club Paradise Roma and shots were on him for the night. Our floor was flooded with strippers and baddies dreaming of snagging a baller. I must admit the Italian women were decent. I've messed around with a few of them, but nothing could compare to a black woman especially my college sweetheart, Cherish.

I think about her more often than I should. On nights like this when I should be turning up and enjoying the perks of being a star, I'd rather be boo'd up. Plenty of times I've contemplated the purpose of remaining overseas when I felt miserable without Cherish and my family. A good girl with morals and values that commands respect and has some business about herself was hard to come by. She was the epitome of wife goals. Too bad I didn't make her my wife.

I tapped my teammate Jeremy on the shoulder, "Let me see your phone really quick." He passed me his Samsung Galaxy S9 with no hesitation. I looked around the club for an area with the less people and maximum privacy, settling for a seat at the far end of the bar. I tapped on the Instagram app, searching for her profile, and clicking on her IG name.

When I decided to take the NBA deal Cherish and I agreed to remain friends, but that arrangement didn't last beyond my flight to Italy. I tried to call her once my plane landed at Ciampino Intl. Airport, but my call went straight to voicemail. Cherish had blocked my number and access to any of her social media accounts. Consequently, I use Jeremy's IG or Facebook to check in on her.

I saw three new pics were added since my last visit. One picture displayed her in a pink dress looking sexy with the caption "SZA After Party". I see she's still a SZA fan after all this time. The next photo contained the fab three hanging out at a restaurant. The last optic showed her sitting behind a desk with the label branch manager on a name plate. I was proud of her. My baby was doing the damn thing. She's always been goal-oriented.

I clicked on the icon that shows the pictures you've been tagged in. To my dismay she was tagged in two beautiful graphics of herself with one of the captions being "Thinkin bout wifin her." I felt my blood boiling as I investigated who this gentleman was. Umph some nigga named Aaron was getting too chummy with her. The comments under the pictures further pissed me off, such as "Damn man that's all you" and "Oouu she bad."

I knew I had no rights to be mad but there was an ounce of hope that she'd wait for me. From the looks of things, the wait was officially over. I locked Jeremy's phone and pulled out my iPhone 8. It was currently 12:38 am meaning it's 6:38 pm in eastern North Carolina, perfect time to catch up with a friend. I searched through my contacts finding the number I was looking for. The person on the other end of the line could better explain who Aaron was and how involved he was with Cherish.

"What's up Dame. It's been a while since I've heard from you. To what do I owe the pleasure for this phone call?"

"Yeah, it's been a minute. I've been busy training for the season. But I'm calling to find out who the hell is Aaron? What's the run down between him and Cherish? How is my baby doing?"

"Really Dame. Just skip past the pleasantries and bombard me with questions. Ugh. Aaron is a business owner of a trucking company. Cherish meet him at the club a couple weeks ago and they recently started dating."

"Have you met him yet?"

"No, not yet but she seems happy. I've always rooted for you two, but…"

"But what Brittish?"

"It's time for her to move on. It's nearing a year and half since you've been gone and it's not fair for her to spend another minute being unhappy. You know how much she's cried and battled with depression. She's content with life. If you love her you'll let the past be the past."

I pulled the phone away from my ear in disbelief at the words coming out of her mouth. I remember us saying periodically during our two years, "Cherish and Dame is a forever thing." Umph, I fucked up big time. I wanted her to be happy, that's all I ever wanted.

"On another note Dame, I don't feel comfortable conversing with you about her personal life. I feel guilty for lying to my best friend and watching her suffer the whole time you've been gone. I can't do it anymore. Cherish will always love you but this is the end--"

I hung up the phone, slamming it down on the bar countertop. I couldn't listen to Brittish's perspective on my relationship with Cherish any longer. She's always been on my team, and now she was switching up. I order two shots of henny from the bartender, taking them straight to the head, back to back.

I felt a hand touch my shoulder, "You good bro?" Jeremy asked. I lied, "Yeah man, let's turn the hell up." I handed him his phone, following him back our section. The DJ started playing "I like it" by Cardi B. One of the pros of being in Italy is they jam to American music. I grabbed one of the best strippers in the building to come over and give me a lap dance.

I pulled out a wad of cash, making it rain on her as she made each booty cheek bounce to the beat of the chorus. She sat down on my groin area placing her hands on my knees for support while she twerked on my dick.

Shawty was doing a sensational job but all I could think about was Cherish. When the song ended I tipped her and dapped up my teammates letting them know I am calling it a night. Valet pulled up my 2017 black BMW 5 series. I headed home in silence to clear my mind. Some way somehow, I was going to win her back. I was going to have to pull an extreme yet strategic move like Dwayne did with Whitley on a Different World. Getting anything done while I was Italy was going to be a challenge, then a lightbulb went off in my head. For Cherish I'm willing to go above and beyond to make things right. The saga of "Cherish and Dame is a forever thing" will happen again if it's the last thing I do.

Chapter 7

Time is Ticking

Brittish

Today was an important day, I'm going wedding dress shopping. Grant gave me his bank card with an unlimited spending budget. I told y'all my future hubby was the best, his career as a stock broker pays very well. I closed the door to my midnight black 2016 Camaro, starting the engine, and getting situated in the driver seat. I had an hour to spare before I was supposed to meet the crew at Elizabella's Bridal and Boutique.

I whipped out of the parking deck, heading towards my favorite Mexican spot, Chipotle. Ten minutes later, "Can I get two bowls to go? I want white rice, no beans, and chicken." I continued to move down the assembly line, checking out, and grabbing some plastic cutlery.

I had one more stop to make before I went to the boutique. I dodged in and out of the hectic lunch rush traffic arriving at Grant's workplace. I was struggling trying to tote my royal blue MK purse and the food and drink carrier while closing my car door.

"Let me help you out Brittish," Derrick said, taking the food and drink, freeing one of my hands. Derrick was one of Grant's co-workers at Intercarolina Financial Services. He was generous for helping me until we reached their office on the second floor.

"Thanks Derrick, I appreciate it." Taking the items out of his arms, sitting them on the receptionist's desk. I knew the receptionist good enough to know she wouldn't mind me borrowing her area briefly.

"No problem, I'm looking forward to the wedding," shortly after Derrick disappeared to his office.

"Most of the company is waiting for the royal wedding," Jessica chimed in. Everybody was counting down till the big day once the save the date invitations revealed the theme was Coming to America. I loved to party so having dancers, a grand entrance, and extensively long wedding train was going to be perfect.

"The entire company better bring a bomb ass wedding gift. Matter fact send out a memo letting everyone know about the gift requirement. Paying for this wedding hasn't been cheap let alone freeloaders attending just to be spectators and give their commentary." The average cost of a wedding is $25k but I have a feeling my wedding will exceed this amount. I don't even know why I'm bitching about the cost when Grant was good for it, no matter how much I decided to spend.

"Oh honey, I know weddings aren't cheap. I watch Four Weddings and Say Yes to the Dress frequently. Plus I was at your engagement party you guys spent a pretty penny," she replied with a sly smile trying to throw some shade. I was used to people commenting on our finances especially single females like Jessica. The chances of meeting a man like Grant didn't occur too often these days.

"Yeah girl, my engagement party was everything I dreamed of thanks to my fiancé." I normally don't feed into the bullshit, but I let Jessica slide with one too many with the slick comments lately.

"Can you page Grant and let him know I'm here?"

"He's gone for the day, hun. He took the rest of the afternoon off. I'm surprised he didn't tell you. I assumed he was going to meet you to handle some wedding plans."

Honestly, I had no idea where he was, but I won't dare let this broad catch me slipping. "Shoot! I forgot he made an appointment to get fitted for his tuxedo. Guess I'll get out of your way. Enjoy your afternoon." I forced myself to smile, gathering everything I strolled in with.

"Bye Brittish, it was good seeing you. Do you need some help, I can get one of the janitors to see you out?" She sounded all bubbly and fake.

"Yes, have somebody meet me on the first floor." I rolled my eyes when I walked away from her desk. Umph. Umph. Umph. Grant was going to hear an ear full from me.

The warm breeze flowing through my car window felt lovely against my tan skin. The shuffle radio on Pandora was projecting through the speakers while I finished my meal. I didn't feel like eating and driving nor waiting to eat once I got to the boutique, which is why I settled for eating in my car.

I cleaned up my mess, throwing the trash and leftover bowl in my backseat. I pressed the phone button on my steering wheel to call Grant, he had some explaining to do.

"Hey wifey, how's your day going?"

"Hey Grant, it's been an interesting day. I'm on my way to try on some dresses."

"Have fun baby. No matter what dress you decide on you'll be the most beautiful bride ever. I would tell you to facetime me during your appointment, but I have an advisory meeting with a client."

"I understand babe. I want you to be stunned when I meet you at the altar anyways. Well I was calling to check in but I'll let you get back to work," I spoke with disappointment in my voice.

"Sounds good babe. Also, I'll be working late tonight, but I'll call you before I head home to see if you need anything. I love you."

"I love you too." I disconnected the call, resuming the music. I know your probably wondering why I didn't set it off like I said I was going to do. I still plan to address my concerns, but I needed to do some investigating first. The fact that he lied so smoothly and even had the nerve to say he would be working late means something was fishy. Grant has never been the lying type and I don't understand why he would start lying now.

I pulled up to the boutique at the same time as my momma and baby sister Dash. I put on my happy face ready to fake it like everything was gravy and biscuits when my mood was far from joyful.

"Hey sissy. You look fabulous." Dash was a younger version of myself from the freckles and slim frame to the burgundy colored hair. The only difference was she had a peanut butter skin tone and wore her hair naturally curly.

I greeted my momma next. The dynamite trio headed into the shop, checking in and waited for the dress consultant. Cherish made her entrance a few minutes later, giving off this glow and happy vibes. The twinkle in her eyes gave me comfort when I thought about how I told Dame to let her be.

"Hello ladies, I'm Emily. I'll be your dress consultant. Which lady is Brittish Simms, the bride to be?" I raised my hand like a school girl to indicate I was the lucky lady.

"Nice to meet you. It was hard to tell who's who. The three of you look like triplets," pointing at my mother, Dash, and me. My mother genes ran deep. The saying "Momma's babies, poppa's maybes" was true for my family, but my daddy knew without a doubt we were his kids.

We all laughed at her comment. I introduced Emily to the crew before we were escorted back to the bridal section. I found a few dresses I wanted to try on and Kenly still hasn't showed up yet. I shrugged the feelings of being upset off with her and Grant. Kenly wouldn't be Kenly if she didn't arrive fashionably late.

Kenly

"Move your ass out of my way" and "Stop your kid from running around the store before I hit them" were my current thoughts as I made a busted through the crowd to reach the self-check section at Wal-Mart. This place was a guaranteed mad house every time I came here. Two people almost backed into me and a few children were almost flat lined by my cart. I had the entire day to run errands, but I was pressed for time due to Brittish's bridal appointment. Who was I kidding, thinking I'd be in and out of here in 15 minutes.

I tapped my foot, humming to myself while I attempted to have patience in this long line. I'm confused on where the traffic was stemming from on a Wednesday afternoon. Finally, the line started moving, I checked out and wheeled my cart to the buggy area. I rushed to grab my three bags racing through the entrance when I fell on my ass from bumping into a stranger.

I looked up wondering what fool wasn't watching where they were going. I just knew my eyes were playing tricks on me when they connected with the person who toppled me over.

"Oh shit, my bad Kenly. Let me help you up," Jaylen said. I haven't seen him since I kicked him out of my apartment a few weeks ago.

"I don't need your help. I got it." I was too prideful to accept his offer. I sat the bags beside me, taking a moment to figure out how I was going to get up.

"Quit being stubborn. Let me help you up." He reached his hand out to me again but this time I decided to take it. I looked ridiculous sitting on the concrete as customers walked around us. I brushed the dirt off my jeans, picked up the bags quickly, and let him know, "Thanks! I appreciate it," before I walked away.

"You're welcome" was all I could hear as the distance between us thicken. I checked the time on my rose gold Apple watch noticing it was pass 3pm, meaning I was super late for the appointment. Fuck it, I never make it anywhere on time anyways.

I unlocked my car doors, putting my stuff in the backseat, and getting my musical selection together before I drove off. I couldn't decide if I wanted to listen to trap rap and be a dope dealer in my mind or play some in my feelings type of music.

A rapid tapping noise begin on the other side of the window putting my search for the perfect song on hold. Low and behold, it was Jaylen. Against my judgement I rolled my window down.

"I'm happy I ran into you. You're looking all good and shit. I miss you Kenly. I never wanted us to end like that. I think what we shared is worth another shot," he voiced with puppy dog eyes.

I did not have time for the bullshit today. "It's funny how you miss me, but I haven't heard from you. Stop lying, you only miss the sex and I promise you you'll never touch this again. And do I look like I'm foolish enough to give you another chance. What we shared was a long-term situationship that should've ended months ago." I sucked my teeth at the audacity of this nigga to expect me to fall for the okie doke again.

"I see your still in your feelings. Regardless of what's happened, I love you."

"Tuhh. I love you too Jay, but I can't do this with you." I reached for my sunglasses. "If you could be gracious enough to back up, I have somewhere I need to be. Unless your cool with getting your retro 11's ran over?" I put the car in drive, leaving him in the parking lot looking stupid like he had me looking for the last year.

***

"I'm here for an appointment with Brittish Simms." The receptionist pointed to her right and told me to look for the bridal section near the back. I took a deep breath, hoping nobody was pissed at my tardiness as I entered the bridal area.

"Well look what the cat drugged in. Take a seat, you haven't missed anything. She's getting ready to walk out in her first dress," Cherish informed me.

I stopped in my tracks staring at her, something was different about her. A good different though, she was glowing or maybe that's the Fenty Beauty highlighter she's wearing. At some point during this visit she had some explaining to do. Momma Simms and Dash wore a resting bitch face with their arms crossed. So much for hoping nobody was mad. I waved in their direction to acknowledge their presence, taking a seat on the red and white striped loveseat next to Cherish.

"Oh my God! My baby! You look stunning!" Brittish's mom cried out. Brittish sported an ivory mesh corset that laced up in the back with a tiered ruffled chapel train. Everybody expressed their opinions on the dress when some tears formed in my eyes. She looked beautiful and deep down in my heart I envisioned myself in a wedding dress get marrying to Jaylen. Despite how I written him off, everything he said to me earlier started playing with my emotions.

"Why are you so emotionally, after being damn near an hour late? If you're going to be late to future appointments, I'm denouncing you as bridesmaid right now." Brittish directed her angry statement towards me.

"I'm sorry I was late. I lost track of time, but I brought you a gift." I retrieved a bottle of champagne and Moscato from my tote. One of the reasons I went to Wal-Mart in the first place was to buy wine. A while back I contacted the boutique to see if alcoholic drinks was permitted and fortunately it was.

"If you thought the option of day drinking would appease me... then you thought right bestie. Pop the bubbly, I'm getting a hubby!" she exclaimed excitedly. Whew thank God I saved my spot as a bridesmaid. The consultant brought us some wine glasses to get things popping. The minute Brittish dropped the attitude, her family did the same. Fixing an issue with Brittish tends to be easy. She didn't stay mad past the moment something happened.

Brittish finished trying on her third wedding dress when she decided to take a break. She strolled out of the fitting area wearing a white silk robe with bride written in blue on the back. She poured herself another glass of wine, seating on the edge of the stage.

"Guess who I ran into when I was rushing to my car trying to get here on time?" This down time was perfect opportunity to fill the girls in. Dash moved from sitting near her mom to kicking it beside Brittish to join the juicy gossip.

"Before y'all start spilling tea worse than the Shaderoom, I'm going to look around the store. Text me when you start trying on dresses again." We all busted out laughing at Momma Simms comment. I thought to myself, what in the world does she know about the Shaderoom.

Once Brittish's mom was out of ear shock I released the true reason behind my tardiness. I filled them in from the moment I ran into Jaylen till I drove off on his immature ass.

"Stop playing girl. Some men will never give up, but I'm proud of you for staying strong." Cherish chimed in. Hearing those words meant so much to me. Cherish always had the will power to leave well enough alone including cutting off her ex-lover. I loved that about her, because my simple ass relied heavily on a man's potential instead of seeing the reality of who he was.

"Thanks love, I'm holding down the promise we made to enjoy being 23. But enough about me. What's been going on with you? You've been checking your phone, smiling and shit. Then you have this black girl magic glow going on."

All eyes fell on Cherish as we waited for her response. Cherish glanced away, taking a sip of champagne. "What are you talking about, Ken?" she recited playfully.

"I did meet a guy at my job that resembled J. Cole. He was fine as hell with grey eyes, but nothing more happened. Outside of that I'm just…happy. Happy with my career. Happy with moving here, just overflowing in happiness."

"Are you sure nothing more happened? Did you have a one-night stand but you're afraid to tell us? I knew those lonely nights with that dildo wasn't cutting it," I commented, answering my own question.

"No bitch! I'm not popping this coochie for anybody. For once life is gucci and my happiness isn't reliant on a man."

Classic Cherish acting like she wasn't studding nobody. We all know sex is conducive for the body and mind. "Okay love, if you say so" dropping the issue and putting an end to the spotlight being on her. Cherish was giddy about something that was deeper than the reasons she was telling us.

"Enough about y'all. Let's get back focused on me." Brittish stood up getting ready to try on more dresses.

"That's the one! This is your wedding dress!" Dash exclaimed, jumping up and down, expressing what we were all thinking. Mrs. Simms gave her stamp of approval wiping her tears away, leaving the final decision up to the bride to be. Brittish eye's glimmered as she took in her appearance through the full-length mirror. "For once I'm agreeing with my sissy, this is my dream dress."

Brittish bodied a sexy white spaghetti strap backless gown that cupped her breast and frame to a tee. The top half of the dress down to her thighs was decorated in lace, followed by a footlong sheer train and veil. The dramatic length was doing the most, but my best friend was stunning in the $15,000 designer gown.

The consultation maneuvered back and forth between Brittish and us to schedule appointments for alterations and future bridesmaid dress fittings on her scheduling app. I bet she was ecstatic for the commission she was going to receive when Brittish handed over the credit card. We're probably their only customers for the day, it's been just us in the building from the moment I walked in.

The minute Mrs. Simms dipped out and the consultation went to handle the transaction, Brittish's entire demeanor changed from upbeat to worried.

"Ladies, I think Grant is cheating on me." Silence filled the air when Brittish dropped her crazy accusations. "I went by his job, but he had left early. He lied to me over the phone saying he's busy at work and he'll be getting off late tonight. He's never lied to me. The only explanation that makes sense is another woman." She paced the floor using her hands to emphasize her concerns. Was this chick serious right now? We didn't spend almost two hours looking and purchasing a wedding dress for a wedding that might get called off.

"The Grant we know wouldn't play you like that. I'm not sure why he lied but hold off on indicting him for something that hasn't been proven yet," Cherish chimed in pulling Brittish in for a sisterly hug.

"Yeah, she's right. Don't jump to conclusions," I mentioned, cosigning everything Cherish said. Brittish and Grant were supposed to be relationship goals, I thought to myself. I promise Grant he would have smoke with the fab 3 plus Dash if he was creeping around on her.

Aaron

I finished printing, signing, and dating a contract, sliding the paperwork over to Romelo. He put his Johnny Hancock on the papers, sending the papers around to the rest of the executive board.

Bing. Bing. **Trina: I seen your new bitch. She's cute, but she ain't me.**

I stared at this dumb ass message in disbelief. I contemplated replying, "Cherish wasn't a bitch and I'm grateful she isn't you." On the other hand, I was in a good mood deciding to leave her on read like the other hoes begging for my attention.

My pops was a proud man, "Congratulations sons. I gave you guys lemons and you made lemonade." My brother and I took the family business a step further by expanding it to moving services. In the next few years the U-Haul business better watch out.

Romelo, I, and the executive board took a group photo for remembrance. "Thank you all for making this endeavor possible. We have our work cut out for us, but in due time this trucking company will put the Ross boys on the Forbes 30 under 30 list," Romelo spoke. I confidently nodded my head in agreeance with my big bro.

The executive board which mainly consumed three shareholders exited the room, leaving only the family and the secretary. I handed the files to my secretary and started chopping it up with my pops and Romelo.

"Carson, don't you see grown men talking? Fax that paperwork, make some business calls. Do the job that we pay you for," I commented to the office secretary.

"Sorry boss. I just wanted to personally congratulate you. Maybe we can celebrate sometime soon," Carson mentioned, batting her eyelashes while she caressed my left arm.

I pushed her hand away, "Thank you, but we won't be celebrating anytime soon." I put my mouth to her ear, "You promised me you wouldn't blur the lines between us. Before I embarrass you, I suggest you get out of my face." Seconds later Carson disappeared like a thief in the night.

I turned my attention back to my family. My father gave me a blank stare, "Ace I taught you to never mix business with pleasure. You're asking for trouble, son."

In my defense, I never intended to smash Carson until we started pulling late hours to finesse this business move. One thing led to another and next thing I know I'm knocking her walls out on top of my desk. For what it's worth, the sex was worth the risk, but I didn't plan to hit it again. Carson was cool but like most girls she expected too much.

"Man, that shit happened weeks ago but your right pops, I've learned my lesson. I'll never touch the help again." I threw my hands up signaling I'm done with her.

"I heard you son, the past is the past and it better stay that way. If you were serious about settling down, I suggest you get your hoes in check now, including little Miss Carson," my father warned me. Carson started to expect too much but I made it clear nothing more would transpire between us. She was the clingy type but she's not malicious.

"I see you Ace, you're coming to your senses about the married life. When did you consider trading in your bachelor card for a loyal beauty?" my brother quizzed me.

I let out a huff, waving them off. "Stop all the marriage and settling down talk. I meet a good girl that's wifey material but that doesn't mean I'm ready to wife her. It's been two and half weeks since we started dating and giving up the player life sounds good but... I don't know man. What I do know is I'm not rushing into anything just yet." I spoke honestly.

"Right now, your straddling the relationship fence. Relationships and marriage add value to a man's life. Only little boys desire to thot forever. If she's a good woman like you say she is, she won't tolerate your bullshit forever. Level up and join the marriage gang sometime soon," Romelo said with my father nodding his gray head in agreement.

I respected Romelo and my father for putting a ring on it but they're suffering from amnesia. Romelo was a renown hoe at NCAT and my dad favorite motto use to be "fuck around before you settle down" meaning have fun before you get out of the player's game.

Knock. Knock. Knock. Carson peaked her head passed the ajar door, "Excuse me Aaron. There's a young lady named Cherish wishing to speak to you. I told her you were busy, but she's adamant and mentioned being your wife. I know she's lying, and I'd be happy to take a message!"

Everybody but Carson let out a laugh. I've jokingly called her wifey before now she's feeding into it. "Don't do that. Transfer wifey to the phone in here," I smirked. Her pretty face transformed into a scowl with a sour tone, "Will do boss." I could sense the jealousy and curiosity over the wifey reference.

The bromance was cut short, sending Romelo back to his office and my father on his merry way. A red light was blinking on line two, "Hey Aaron, I'm sorry to bother you at work but I couldn't reach your cell phone. It's nothing important but I wanted you to meet my friends." Her angelic voice sounded through the phone, and I took my phone out of my pants pocket noticing it was dead. "You're not bothering me, I'm happy to hear from you. My phone died, and I'm cool with meet your homegirls.

"How does tomorrow night sound?" She sounded eager for me to meet her friends.

"I should be free and if I'm not I'll clear my evening schedule just for you beautiful."

"Thanks! I'll call you later with the details. Work hard and enjoy the rest of your day."

It's nearing 4pm and I'm feeling tapped out on working. I've been busting my ass for months with Carson's assistance and approval from Romelo who's the president to pull this new business venture off. I'm glad the board signed off on this idea reducing my stress level.

Bing. Bing. **Nikki: Come through tonight, I haven't seen you in a few days.**

Bing. Bing. **Liv: Why are you avoiding me? That chick from IG has you tripping. You know you miss this pussy and spit game.**

My response to the two of them was: **I'm out of town handling some business.**

Nikki was a caramel big booty chick and Liv was one of my sister-in law associates. I've been fucking Nikki on and off over the last year and a half. Whereas, Liv was newbie to my rooster. Between these broads and thinking about the business expanding soon I was encountering a headache. Lord knows I saw a future with Cherish but having different women for different needs enticed me.

The wonderful thought of vacationing on the beach soothed my mind. "Fuck it" I said to myself, I'm taking a few days off to relax. I phoned Carson, "I need you to handle a couple of things for me. First, clear my schedule from tomorrow afternoon to the following Monday. Second, find a hotel preferable a couple's suite and book a flight for two at a location with a beach."

Carson was the company's secretary, but I often treated her like my personal assistant. "I'll get on it, but do you realize it's a short notice to be going out of town and canceling meetings." She voiced her opinion with a nasty attitude.

My dad had a value point, I need to get my hoes in check and looks like the first one will be Carson. "I sense your feathers are still roughed up from earlier, but Carson you're not my woman and let's not forget who's the boss in this bitch. You've been trying me today, stay in your lane and don't question a boss. Email me the info by midnight." I hung up the phone not caring if I hurt her feelings. Females these days really know how to piss a nigga off. I'm looking forward to this getaway with my leading lady.

Chapter 8

Love Birds

Brittish

"Babe, I want a cartoon drawing of us. Let's get one done while we wait on the other half of our double date to show up." I started whining in Grant's ear knowing he'd do whatever I asked for.

Grant and I studied the five drawers and selected the best one to do a color filled replicate of us. Grant sat down in the black foldout chair with his legs wide open. I gracefully positioned myself on his lap, draping my arm around his neck, and let my feet hang in between the free space of his legs. I brought my face closer to his with all 32's showing for the artist to begin our masterpiece.

It felt like the drawing was taking forever and staying still was getting tiresome. The sound of railroad tracks shaking from the roller coasters, kids running around screaming, and the smell of funnel cakes filled my nostrils. All the excitement around us was making me antsy to enjoy the Carolina Central festivities.

In the nick of time our artist finished the drawing right before Cherish called my phone. Grant paid for the portrait, then we walked to the front entrance.

"Hey boo, this is Aaron. Aaron this my best friend Brittish and her fiancé Grant." I eyed him up and down giving Cherish a fist bump letting her she picked a winner. Two baddies with two chocolate men,

I think yes! I could see Aaron and Cherish being a force to reckon with if they made things official.

We chatted for a bit then decided on how many tickets we should buy. The first ride of the night was a mini version of the drop zone. No matter how fast the drop went Cherish and I couldn't help but scream like little kids.

We convinced the guys to go for a few rounds on the ferris wheel. Aaron was a smooth character for bringing an overdue smile and happiness to Cherish's life. Having a man isn't everything but my girl needed some loving. What's the point of going through life without having somebody to share it with. I squeezed Grant's hand feeling grateful I had met the man I was going to spend a lifetime with.

Aaron helped Cherish clean up her powdery face. The strawberry funnel cake we shared had gotten everywhere. I wiped some white residue off my dress. The evening was going good until Grant stepped away to answer a phone call. My insecurities surfaced, and a negative gut feeling plagued my stomach. Grant went missing for quite some time or at least that's how long it seemed. We had time to clean up the table and Aaron brought Cherish some cotton candy before he came back to join us.

I wanted to play it cool but nah fuck that. "When did we start being secretive with our phones. You've had one too many calls in private lately?" I divulged, not taking my eyes off him. He looked back at me dumbfounded, ugh niggas love to act like they don't know what's going on.

"Don't look like that. I've noticed how suddenly refuse to take calls from work when we're together. Then you lied about being at work several days ago. Care to explain yourself?"

Tension was as thick as a smoked turkey leg. Cherish made a face with her lips poked out pleading for me to drop the subject, while Aaron held her by the waist and focused his attention on the people walking pass us. The clouds grew to a darker grey hue as I waited impatiently on an answer.

"What do you mean Brittish? It was noisy, so I walked away. Nothing more, nothing less. When did you become the phone call police?"

I undercrossed my arms, pacing back and forth on the concrete feeling an invisible smoke steaming from my ears. He deliberately ignored my accusation regarding work. Cherish grabbed my hand, "Let's drop this conversation and prepare to blow our lungs out on this next ride." I gathered my thoughts but letting this shit go wasn't an option. "I became the cell phone monitor when my finance started ly—" my sarcastic sense of humor came to an end when a loud crackle followed by lighting lit up the sky.

Aaron suggested we call it night before the storm hit. We said our goodbyes and I beat Grant to the car. I should've locked him out of his own black Range Rover. I picked up my phone to send a text to Cherish, letting her know I hated our double date was cut short. Our next girl's chat should be interesting.

Vroom. Beep. Beep. Pitter-patter. Screechhhh. My eyes widen as the Range Rover came to a screeching halt, Grant almost tapped the back of a white Ford Focus. "My fault Britt. Are you good babe?" he asked me. I nodded my head up and down refusing to speak to him. Between the weather and congestion on I-40, getting home was turning into a pure headache. Now we're stuck in a standstill in the middle lane. I rested my head against the glass, closing my eyelids as I contemplated the future of this relationship. I turned around facing Grant, resting my left elbow on the center console and chin onto my slight opened fist.

"Are you cheating on me? Please, be honest. I wouldn't ask you this if I didn't want to hear the truth?" I inhaled a deep breath mentally preparing for the worst.

He's gazes meet my prominent eyes. "No! I'm not cheating. I promise on everything I love I'd never disrespect you like that.". Deep down in my heart I wanted to believe him, but my mind knew something wasn't adding up.

"Umph. If you're not cheating hand over your phone, now!". Grant pressed the gas pedal moving us up another mile as traffic started to ease up.

He grasped my hand while keeping his focus on the highway. "Brit, I need you to trust the fact that I'm not fucking around. It's not necessary to rummage through my phone."

"Tuhhh. You're kidding right?" I snatched my hand away feeling tempted to slap his black ass. "You're so full of shit! Everybody thinks your fiancé of the year, but that's a lie! Grant takes good care of you. He's so in love. Blah. Blah. Blah. Bullshit!" I couldn't contain my hands anymore, punching him in the arm to release some pented up anger.

"If you hit me again I'm going to take the next exit and handle your spoiled ass," He stated calmly.

Whack! My fist connected to his muscular chest. Whack! I jabbed him in his side too. I don't condone violence, lord knows I don't, but this situation was bringing out the worst in me. I stopped hitting him when my knuckles started aching. However, Grant ate my punches without flinching thanks to his rock-hard muscles. He continued to piss me off with his calm demeanor and ignoring my antics. True to his word he took the next exit.

"I want to go home! Take me home nowww!" I whined. He whipped into Burger King's scarce parking lot. He backed into one of the parks that was surrounded by trees creating a division between the lot and highway. He killed the head lights, jumped out the car, and snatched open the passenger door.

"You've been talking shit for the last ten minutes. Get your ass out of the car!"

Oh, shit I thought to myself. I wonder if he was going to beat me like Chris did RiRi, maybe he was going to put me out and drive off, or worst what if he kills me. I mentally counted to ten to before I stepped out of the car. He really must be feed up with my shit, I've never heard him raise his voice at me.

I posted up against the car door hoping a BK worker would call the police if things went left. He walked up close enough to the point where he could smell me breathing, making me flinch. He placed his hands on both sides of me boxing me in as he hovered over me.

"You want to argue and fight for what though? Your trying to pull some shit you've seen on your little ratchet reality shows, hoping to get a reaction out of me." Damn he was reading my ass like an open book. "Listen here, I understand your in your feelings but I'm not cheating," some fresh tears hit my cheeks and he wiped them away for me.

"I love you Grant, I swear I do, but if I find out your up to no good this engagement is cancelled, and we'll be attending your funeral instead."

He busted out laughing but I didn't see nothing funny. "Man, I don't know who's the craziest? Your crazy ass for threaten to kill me or me for I still wanting to marry you." I shook my head he had a value point.

"It's all good Brittish, I'm not sweating it. Stop acting like a spoiled brat spazzing out with temper tantrums and shit and start acting like my soon to be wife."

I tilted my head to the side to avoid meeting his lips, he wasn't getting off that easy. He settled for kissing my cheek, working his way down my neck with a trail of sensational kisses. We engaged in a make out session like two horny teenagers. The sexual tension was heating up as he cupped my cheeks.

Grant climbed into the backseat motioning me to join him. I straddled his groin area, unfastening his pants while he lifted my dress, ripping my panties off in one swift gesture. I gripped his manhood with my dick clincher nails, sliding down his pole inch by inch. Grant's coarse hands held my hips, pounding my insides out with every deep stroke he administered. From the corner of my eye I saw the windows fogged up. He nibbled on my ear whispering, "I love you."

I screamed out "I love you too baby!" as I creamed on his dick. Moments later he went limp inside of me releasing his seeds.

I hopped off Grant, stretching my arm pass the center console to the glover compact in search of some napkins to clean us up. Our hostile moment was massacred, but an uneasy feeling still lingered in my spirit.

I felt like a weak bitch for caving into his charm, but like I've been telling him all along, "What's done in the dark comes to the light."

Cherish

Ding. Ding. Ding. Aaron's phone ringing interrupted our conversation. I glanced at the touch screen to see his mother was calling. I could feel my anxiety kicking in as racing thoughts filled my mind, wondering if he would answer or has he told his mother about me. My thoughts were put to rest when he pressed a black button on the steering wheel.

"Hey momma."

"Hey Aaron, are you too busy to do your mother dearest a favor?" It was evident she was a sweetheart from the tone of her voice. I bet I'd like her if I was given the chance to meet her.

"Well, I'm riding in the car with Cherish. She can hear you by the way, but what did you need me to do?"

Instead of answering his question she spoke to me. "Hey sweetie, you're the lovely lady that has my son acting different. It's good to know he wasn't lying to me."

"Mom don't start!" Aaron stated sternly before I could speak for myself.

"Childdd, did you forget you were talking to your mother? Don't make me embarrass your black ass."

To lighten the tension between those two I addressed Mrs. Ross previous comments. "Hey Mrs. Ross, yes it's me! Aaron wasn't lying to you."

Aaron squeezed my hand hard and side eyed me suggesting I didn't need to say anything else. I wonder why he's trying to hush me up.

"So, mom what favor did you want me to handle?" he sounded annoyed.

"Can you go by my house and set the alarm. We were rushing out of the house so fast to catch a last-minute flight to New York and neither one of us remembered to enable the alarm system."

"I'll take care of it after I drop Cherish off. Be safe and enjoy your trip." His mother thanked him and said her goodbyes to us.

Travis Scott latest album crooned through the car. The fair was fun, but I was beyond grateful to see the silver gates opening, leading the way to Aaron's condo. I grabbed my purse and Aaron grabbed my PINK diamond stubbed black tote and black luggage from the trunk.

The car engine stayed running as I followed him up the stairs, thanking him for carrying my bags. Too many men these days depend on the woman to do everything for themselves.

"You don't have to thank me, it's a man's job to take care of his lady." He smiled, inserting his key and letting us in.

"When did I become your lady? I don't recall agreeing to that." I questioned him trying to suppress my happiness at the thought of being solely his. He left me looking dumbfounded when he continued to carry my bags to their destination. I stepped out of my shoes, not wanting to track dirty up the carpeted staircase.

I reached the top landing while he was preparing to walk back down. He examined my face knowing something was bothering me. Sometimes I hated how my facial expressions always revealed my true feelings.

"I didn't mean to leave you hanging. Let's save that discussion for later once I returned from my parent's place. Make yourself at home. I brought your favorite wine and snacks and set up the guest room per your request. If you anything while I'm out don't hesitate to call me."

Let me give you the run down real quick. Aaron asked me to go out of town with him for the weekend after we made plans to go to the fair and I foolishly agreed. Spending the weekend with somebody was a big deal and quite frankly we haven't established a title yet. Being in close quarters with a male after being alone for an extensive time felt odd, which is why I wanted to sleep in separate beds. Ideally, I should've stayed home and drove over the next day for our getaway, but he convinced me otherwise. He was holding me hostage from society until Sunday afternoon.

"Thanks for respecting my wishes. I'm going to soak in the tub and enjoy some Roscato." He brushed his lips against mine giving me a lustful lip lock. A pleasurable sensation coursed through my body until he pulled away.

"See you in a few."

✳✳✳

I ransacked his cabinets for a wine glass, pouring myself a glass of red wine. I headed back upstairs before the bath I was running overflowed. The piping hot water mixed with a cotton candy bath bomb created a purple sea in the freestanding tub. I turned some music on, slipped out of my clothes, and settled into tub.

My toes started to have creases and the water was turning cold from the amount of time I laid in their soaking. I got out to dry my body off in a expensive white towel. Even his choice in towels was above and beyond the regular standards. I swallowed my last sip of wine, tuning out the sucking noise of the water draining.

I tucked in the front of the towel underneath my arm before I headed downstairs. I went into the kitchen pouring myself another glass of wine and connected my phone to his bluetooth system. The lush carpet meshed with my polished manicured feet as I waltzed around sipping my wine and making myself at home.

Drip. Drip. Drip, I was in the mist of singing *Boo'd Up* when the bottom of the sky fell out. I turned down the music, stumbling over to the glass window. Clearly, the wine was settling in.

I looked out into the rainy sky feeling a sense of happiness wash over me. I don't know if it was the wine, the weather, or whatever but happiness was taking over me. For the first time in a long time I was genuinely happy without Dame. He was my first love, but I think I'm ready to be serious with Aaron. I know I categorized him as another ain't shit nigga, but maybe I was wrong. I made a mental note to ask Grant what he thought about him. A quality man can always spot out another quality man.

I need to put on my matching short set before Aaron gets back but the clammy scenery through the glass was intriguing. When my lease is up I need to find an apartment with a window view like this, it's everything.

"Enjoying the view, Chocolate."

Damn, he's back already. I slightly turned around to see his face, "Yes I am. You know I'm obsessed with the window view."

"If you'd stop playing with a nigga you could have a window view whenever you wanted."

His broad chest touched my back, and he kissed my shoulder. My lady parts started to get moist while heat radiated through my body. I could feel his dick rising and my hormones jumping. Wine tends to make me hot, hungry, or horny, and right now I was hot and horny.

He wrapped one arm around my waist, whispering in my ear "I want you in the worst way."

I took a deep breath… "Too bad you can't have me right now." If only I would have taken my ass upstairs sooner and changed, I wouldn't be in this predicament. That damn wine had me ready to get loose as a goose, but I remembered why I took a hiatus from sex.

"I need some space," removing myself from his arms, attempting to get away from him. He was faster than me, placing both his hands on the window boxing me in.

"Cherish, I told you I want you to be mine." I swallowed the lump in my throat avoiding his glaze, and the faint sound of Rihanna "Yeah I Said It" circulated in the air. I felt like we were playing the childhood game of freeze tag since neither one of us made a move.

I was nervous as hell when he dropped down to his knees. He proceeds to open the bottom of my towel coming face to face with my freshly waxed kitty. "I don't want to do this Aaron," I pleaded. Deep down inside I really wanted too, but good girls don't fuck this soon.

"I won't do anything to you that you don't want me to do. Can I taste it?"

Not waiting for an answer, he held my thighs apart placing kisses on my clit, making me shutter. "Damn you taste good," he said talking to my box.

"Do you want me to stop?" he asked me, using his tongue to lick between my folds in a circular motion causing a wet sensation to leak out instantly. Got damn I missed this feeling, it's been too long.

"Cherish is this what you want?" tapping my thigh to get my attention.

Fuck it. I looked down getting memorized with his eyes, "Yes!" I'm going against the grain and I'll deal with the consequences late. I have needs and Aaron is ready to satisfy them.

"Put your leg over my shoulder." I did as I was told but feared I would fall trying to depend on one leg.

"Don't look like that, I got you. You're not going to fall." He gripped my right leg from behind and wrapped his arm around my other thigh. He put his mouth over my pearl sucking on my clit, licking around my vaginal opening. "Shit, Aaron" I held onto my towel hoping it doesn't fall. My legs got weak, when he went back to slurping on my love bud. I tried to push his head away, but he wasn't having it. "Aaron, I'm cumminggg!" exploding moments later.

He got up, giving me a sloppy kiss letting me taste myself while I sucked on his bottom lip. I helped him take off his shirt and he ripped my towel off. He toyed with my nipples, fixing his mouth to say, "Are you going to return the favor?" Normally, the answer would be hell no but I'm dropping the good girl act for the night and I might as well go all in.

I pulled his pants and Ralph Lauren briefs down, taking his manhood in my hands, slowly slipping my lips around the tip. He held the back of my head inching his dick in my mouth. I bobbed my head up and down, spitting on it and everything. "Yes babe, suck it like you mean". I increased my speed to the point where my jaws were getting sore. For somebody who hated sucking dick and only did it to Dame on occasions, I was giving Aaron an award-winning show.

He pulled out, "Enough of this foreplay shit."

Stepping out his bottoms, he hoisted me up against the glass and I wrapped my legs around him for security. He guided his dick inside me while kissing my lips and neck. I briefly felt uncomfortable waiting for my walls to stretch out a bit. Aaron was big man compared to me and his dick proved to be no different as he took control of my pussy.

"Damn your gripping the hell out of my dick."

"Mmmm, I told you, mmm... it's been a while," I managed to say between breathes. He pounded in and out of me slowly, almost to the beat of the rain hitting the glass. I carved my coffin shaped nails into his back. He grabbed my face looking me in the eyes, "I want you to be mine." My pussy let out a noise like she was responding back to his statement for me. My second orgasm was building up, "Aaron I'm 'bout to cum again."

"Not yet baby. Bend over and touch your toes," he commanded, letting me out of his grasp. Thanks to my vigorous dance experience I could touch my toes with ease or at least until he ran his dick up in me. The infamous sound of mac and cheese could be heard as he hit it from the back.

"I can't wait any longer Aaron.!"

"Fuck Cherish" he proclaimed speeding up his stroke game. My juiced steeped out running down my leg just as he pulled out and finished on my right ass cheek.

Got damn, I forgot how good busting a nut felt on a real dick instead of the plastic shit I've been rocking with.

Aaron

I pulled the oven baked bacon from the stove, stirred the grits, and poured two glasses of orange juice. I was grinning from ear to ear this morning your boy got some cuddy last night and the shit was amazing.

I walked into my bedroom noticing she was sleeping still. "Cherish, cherish," I whispered in her ear placing kisses over her face. "Good morning sleepy head."

She sat up in bed gaining her composure. A nigga was feeling nice as hell to be feeding her breakfast in bed like she was baby already.

"Last night was epic", she mentioned in-between chewing her food.

"Yes it was sweet cheeks." I slapped her thigh through the bedspread. We spent some time eating and laying around before, I put our packed bags in the trunk preparing for the airport traffic to be booming on Friday. This trip was for pleasure and maybe some business if the opportunity presented itself.

The sunny Miami weather blessed my skin when we walked outside to wait for our driver to drop us off at the Ritz Carlton. Carson was a pain in the ass, but she booked a great getaway for the weekend.

"You did all this for me Aaron? This ocean view suite is nice as hell."

"When it comes to you just name the price and it's yours."

Cherish had me doing things out of my comfort zone. I've never taken a female on a baecation and shawty got me spending guap on her pretty ass. I'm not saying money was an issue but outside of my momma no other woman had me acting like such a gentleman.

I was starving like Marvin waiting for Cherish to freshen up in the bathroom. I ordered two burgers and fries from room service. It was straight, but the Ritz could step up their cooking skills a bit.

"Hurry up Cherish before your food gets cold." I swear women can take forever to get ready. Even a simple outfit change was taking her a minute.

"There goes my chocolate goddess." My baby was rocking a white mesh two-piece high waisted swim suit. Her breasts were on full display as well as her booty, I reached out slapping one of her sweet cheeks. Cherish has a slight pudge which concerned her, but nothing could take away from her beauty.

I changed into a red pair of Burberry swimming trunks remaining shirtless and Cherish put on her gold PINK slides. We got down to the pool area right on time for happy hour. We ordered drinks, posted up in the lounge chairs on some king and queen type shit.

"Aaron, thank you for everything." She switched from her chair to straddling my waist as I laided back.

"I thought after Dame nobody could compare to him, but I was wrong. Then I thought you might've been another fuck nigga, but you keep proving me wrong."

Cherish was green to some things but I had her just where I wanted her. I kissed her breast, using my right thumb to hold her bottoms to the right side of her lips, playing in between her folds. She was catching my vibe when she whipped my dick out and sat down on it. We were coupled up under a large palm tree which made our area darker than the rest of the pool scene.

Geez..neither one of us cared about catching a indecent exposure charge as she rode the magic stick, throwing her head back when I started pounding her from underneath.

Jared

I counted the safe at the trap house before I put my deposit inside. I sold my last and final two bricks meaning I'm cashing out this weekend and officially out of the game.

I put $15k inside the safe, keeping $35k for myself. The dope money was good while it lasted. I had over six figures stashed away under one of the floor panels at my grandma house. If somebody ever tried to rob the place they'd run out of patience looking for the stash.

"I didn't understand at first but I'm proud of you Jared. This street life isn't for everybody. If you ever fall short Roman is willing to put you back in the game." I thanked my homie Malik for everything he did from childhood until I got straighten out from my prison stint.

My life was transitioning before my eyes from a dope dealer to a government job as a banker, who would've thought I'd end up here. Every time I thought about the bank I wondered about Cherish and ole' boy. I should've got some gang bangers to rough his preppy ass up for talking shit but the new me was a changed man. I wasn't allowing nothing else to send me back in the pen.

Boom! Boom! Boom! Rounds of gunshots bombarded the trap house. I ducked behind the couch pulling out my GLOCK 17. I peeked out briefly realizing a group of men dressed in all black and ski mask was trying to rob the crew. Who knew about this location beside the team was clouding my mind. I shook off the thoughts knowing somebody wasn't going to make it out of here alive.

I jumped up from behind the couch emptying my clip ultimately taking out two of the robbers. The other person made a run for it out the front door. I chased after him but lost him when he raced into the brushes.

Fuck! Who was gunning for the squad like that, maybe Malik had an idea of who those niggas were. I slammed the screen door walking into the living room making sure Malik was good.

"Jared, Jared. They got me man." Malik was spitting out blood on the brown carpet and holding one of the multiple gunshot wounds that imping his body. I took out my phone ready to call 911 for the second time in my lifetime.

"Don't call the police man, just promise me you'll take care of my daughter and Slim." Slim was his baby momma and high school sweetheart. I shook my head in agreeance. I missed some of his daughter's toddler years but long as I had breath in my body she'll never want for everything.

I held him in my arms trying to stop him from shaking and bleeding out, but the blood was pouring out like a stream. Moments later his bodily movements came to a halt. He's lifeless body fell limp in my arms, a lone tear cascaded down my face.

Life was on the way up, but some bullshit always had to happen. Feeling this type of lost fueled my animosity to seek revenge. If you live by the gun, die by the gun.

Chapter 9

Acquaintances

Cherish

"Hey Aaron, it's Cherish. I was calling to see how your mom was doing. Give me a call back when you can. I miss you." I felt disappointed again as I ended the concerned voicemail.

Everything was all good about a week ago, but since we returned from the beach, Aaron's been acting funny. I don't know what's his deal, but we had a good time fucking and exploring Miami. We made plans to get together this past Tuesday, but he cancelled on me when he's mom was rushed to the ER from food poisoning. I felt horrible for his mom, but it's been two days and he's still acting distance. I could be tripping but my intuition suspected something deeper was going on.

I put my phone on the charging, sliding out of bed into my black slippers to start my morning routine before work. I was in the mist of letting my clean and clear facial wash hydrate my hershey skin, when self-guilt settled in. I thought to myself "You shouldn't have given up the cookie up that soon. He probably thinks you're no different than other women. He probably has a woman already. I should pop up at his job. What if he's secretly married. Nah, what if he's a scammer. Nah. Ugh." Multiple thoughts raced through my mind but the idea of popping up on him stuck with me the most.

According to my apple watch it's 7:45 in the morning, I had a little over an hour to get to the office. I danced around the house throwing clothes everywhere eventually settling for some black slacks, a golden long sleeve sheer blouse, and maroon colored booties. I loved a good color block vibe for the fall. Within 30 minutes I was hopping in the car and merging into the hectic I-40 traffic to my destination.

✳✳✳

I adjusted the top button of my silk blouse allowing my girls to be the center of attention. I secretly thanked Victoria Secret for their push-up bra.

"Excuse me miss, I'm here to see Aaron Ross."

"Can I get your name? I schedule all his meetings and appointments, and nobody under the name of Cherish was put on his calendar for this morning. Sorry ma'am!" this broad had the nerve to say. I flipped my hair with my left hand channeling my inner bitch side.

"Listen sis, I know all about you just like you've made it your business to know about me. I'm Cherish Wright, the one who told you I'm wifey the last time I called up here! Don't play dumb—"

In the nick of time Aaron graced us with his presence and another fine specimen who resembled him was standing not too far behind him. "Hey ladies, what's going on here?" he kissed me on the cheek and half hugged me. His vibe was off, but from the look on Carson's face it was enough to piss her off.

"Carson and I were getting acquainted, but I stopped by to see you."

"Aight, cool. Carson knows better than to be giving wifey a hard time." I felt giddy on the inside, this bitch better learn her place quickly.

"It's a pleasant surprise to see you. Let's head back to my office."
He placed his hand on the small of my back, pushing me down the
hallway.

On the way to his office I was introduced to the fine gentlemen
who turned out to be his older brother. He handed Aaron a stack of
papers, "I need you to sign some papers and get Carson to handle it
from there. It was nice to meet you Cherish. You're as beautiful as he
described you to be. I'll holla at you later Ace." They dapped each
other up and he made sure to close the door on his way out.

I felt myself blushing, this nigga done told the family about me
well technically just his brother, maybe I didn't fuck him too soon. I
paraded around his office bullshitting around the reason I decided why
I popped up on him.

"Cherish stop playing games and tell me the real reason for your
visit."

I bit my bottom lip, "Well…I felt like you've been ignoring me
until just now. I know your mom got sick and I may sound selfish but
what about me? You've gotten me out of my element from knocking
my walls down to having me doing pops up. Ughh I should've never
done this!" I grabbed my Michael Kors bag preparing to leave. I felt
and sounded pressed for a man who once upon a time checking for me
more than I was checking for him.

"Wait love!" he grabbed my hand to stop me from leaving. "I'm
sorry I've been preoccupied with my mom. I wasn't purposely trying
to ignore you. I care about you and you should never question that. I
told you I'm a man of my words."

He seems sincere, but his actions will be the true test. "My mom is
supposed to come home tomorrow. I'm going to help my dad get her
squared away but, in the meantime, how about you schedule a spa day

with your homegirls courtesy of me. I know how ladies like to spend the week of and before to prepare for GHOE."

GHOE is the greatest homecoming on earth hosted by A&T. I wasn't an aggie breed and I rep my alma mater but anybody with good sense participated in the festivities. This is my first time experiencing GHOE but the word around town is the city is on party mode for a week. I'm just wondering will homecoming bring out the hoe in some people.

After checking out my nails I gladly accepted his offer. This spa day would be the perfect way to let Kenly in on mysterious happiness. He pulled out one of his credit cards from his wallet handing it over to me while smoothly sneaking in a kiss.

"Babe stop I'm running late for work," I whined.

He slapped my ass, "You knew what you were doing when you came over here in those tight ass pants. There's only one way your leaving out of here." He gave me a seductive look as he locked his office door.

I sent Tori a text letting her know I would be late as usually. Aaron undid his pants as I stepped out of my heels. I leaned over the table taking a quick look back at him before he slid it in. Something about skin on skin contact took sex to another level. He kissed my neck, massaging my clitoris between his fingers as he gave me a much-needed morning workout.

Kenly

I walked into A to Zen Massage, giving the receptionist Cherish's name. Minutes later I was in the locker room changing into nothing but an all-white robe with a gold A-Z emblem.

I entered the private room that was reserved for us to see Cherish and Brittish kekeing during their pedicure. I settled into the massage chair, moving my feet around in the steamy hot water.

"Lee Lee, can you add a tab bit of cold water please?" Brittish and Cherish fall out laughing,

"Kenly why are you calling her Lee Lee, every foreign person isn't named that."

"Girl you know how I am with the nicknames; I didn't mean anything by it." Although it was a joke, I apologized to the masseuse and made a mental note to stop referring to foreign women as Lee Lee.

I sipped on some wine and allowed the soft melodies to soothe my mind. The past two weeks Jaylen has been trying to wiggle his way back in, but I was holding strong for now. I often wished he could be the man I believed him to be a long time ago. I shrugged the disappointing thought away.

"Cherish, spill the tea and don't lie either. You've been glowing for a while now and out of the blue your offering to pay for a spa day. What's the deal sis?"

Classic Cherish tried to avoid the question but like white on rice I wasn't letting up. "I mean I'm enjoying my promotion and felt like celebrating that's it, nothing more, nothing less."

"Bitch, please. Something is up and clearly Brittish knows something too because she's quiet as a church mouse. One of you better start talking and quick. We don't do hold nothing back in our circle."

Splash, splash. The sound of the water being thrown on our legs consumed the atmosphere as I continued to wait for an answer.

"Well I was going to tell you sometime today, but I meet somebody. His name is Aaron. He's a successful business owner of a trucking company but most importantly he's the reason I'm treating us to a spa day. He paid for all of this."

I knew something was different about her. Sis went from being down and out to a blossoming flower. I'm happy for my girl she deserves it after everything she went through with Dame no good trifling ass. Brittish was a fan of his but I didn't care for him like that.

"Cherish why didn't you tell meee! That's why your ass was smiling and shit at Brittish dress fitting. Yes sis, get your groove back. It's new nigga season." I said playfully dancing in the massage chair.

"Did Brittish already know?" I questioned.

"Sorry Ken, yes Brittish already knew and she's meet him too. I was hesitant to tell you since your situation with Jaylen is what it is now."

It felt like a slap in the face that she told Brittish before she told me, and she let her meet him already. We're all best friends but I always felt somewhat closer to Cherish despite our ongoing love hate moments. Yeah, my situation with Jaylen is fucked up but that didn't mean I didn't want to hear how happy everybody else was with their love life. I wanted to express my feelings about this hidden information but now wasn't the time.

"I understand love and Cherish don't judge me, but I'm itching to know have you let him hit yet? I mean most men don't sponsor anything unless it's something in it for them." I sounded rude but it's 2018, no nigga ain't paying for shit if he's not getting something.

"Damn Ken, let me know what you really think about me. You know I've never been pressed for somebody else's money. I can't believe you would have the nerve to say some bullshit like that."

Shit, I sounded like a hater without meaning too. This broad has somebody breaking bread on her ass after a few weeks if it's been that long, yet Jaylen thought I should be content with good dick and occasionally going on dates. I shouldn't be comparing my situation to hers, but she knew what she wanted and refused to settle for less. Too many times, I silently judged her for choosing to be alone yet she's the one with the prince in armor while I've been looking stupid.

"I'm sorry Cherish, I didn't mean it like that. I know you're not that type of chick. I was out of line for saying that."

Brittish started cracking jokes to lighten the mood. "Damn y'all bitches get on my nerve being in your feelings. Cherish all Ken wants to know are you sexing him yet? And Ken, there is somebody who will love you the right way, keep putting the Jaylin bullshit behind you. Now hug it out, kiss and make-up! I'm trying to enjoy my moment of spending somebody else's money beside my own on that expensive ass wedding."

"Britt your man has hella money stop the broke bitch act." We busted out laughing in unison and cracked open another bottle of wine while the masseuses finished up polishing our toes.

"Well Ken the answer to your question is yes, but I feel like it happened too soon," Cherish blabbed out quickly.

"Yassss honey!" Brittish and I expressed at the same damn time.

"Don't feel bad now, you've already rode his dick. We're grown, and sex is innate. Getting your rocks off is good for the soul boo. So, how was it sis? Did he give you that act right? Give me details." Although, the green jealousy monster was weighing heavy on me, I lived for a bomb sex story.

"Y'all he wore my ass out during round one. I forgot how good sex could be. For a minute I felt like a virgin again but once he started pounding my walls in I was grateful for every inch of dick that was hitting my spot. He's perfect, almost too perfect. I like him, but I don't know—"

I cut her off before she could compare him to Dame. He's a blast from the past and it needed to stay that way. "Look sis, don't give up a good man because you're having doubts. He's not Dame, no man will ever be him but he's treating you right and seems to be dicking you down correctly," I interjected. Cherish and I were totally opposites. She was quick to cut any nigga off that paid her some mind after Dame left.

"Yeah, he's seems perfect which is something Grant noticed too, but until he gives you a reason to think otherwise enjoy the moment. Trust your gut it never steers you wrong," Britt chimed in.

"Okay, okay. I'll chill and give it some time."

"Good, this situation could teach you how to have patience. Now enough self-doubt what does he look like?"

Cherished searched through her phone for a picture, showing me a dark-skin man wearing a black shirt displaying his muscular physic. "Okay, sis he's fine. I see you boo. I hope I'll meet him soon."

"If he continues to act right he'll be meeting you and maybe other important people in my life." A smile graced her face as she talked about him. Brittish was getting married, Cherish was dating, and then there's me, alone for the first time in my life since I started dating in high school.

Aaron

Bad bitches only, bad bitches on me (bad)

Bad bitches only, bad bitches on me

BBO by Migos boomed through the surround sound system in my brother's man cave. A few of the guys came over to watch the first NBA game of the season.

"Ace turn that degrading music down before I kick you out of my house," Gina commanded. "Chill, G it's just a song. You know how the boys get down when we get together."

"Nigga please you're the only one in this crew that disrespects females and have a rooster of hoes. I pray I live to see the day where you find value in women. Women are more than sex objects and for every female you've done wrong there's a list of karma waiting to get your ass," she continued to her rant while setting up the food for the night. Outside of popping her gums, my sister-in law could cook. She prepared lemon pepper and mild wings, cheeseburger sliders, mozzarella sticks, and beer.

I gave Romelo a looking hoping he'd get his wife to shut the hell up, but he was sucka ass nigga when it came to Gina. In his mind whatever Gina says goes and hell will freeze over became he disagrees with his wife. Whenever I wife Cherish she'll know her place unlike Gina.

I grabbed a corona from the fridge attempting to drown out her voice during the remainder of the pool game, but the shit wasn't working. I hit the end of my pool stick on the ground.

"Damn Gina I get it. Black women are everything. I know I'm a fuck nigga at heart, but a special lady has come into my life and I'm trying to change me. So please stop saying I don't value black women because I do, but I often value being a nigga more." I stated angerly. In my defense the women I mess with knows I'm not shit except for Cherish. She's special and I'm doing my best to keep my doggish ways hidden from her.

The reflection on my brother's face and Gina's "oh no you didn't" black woman stance let me know I was better off not replying to her simple ass the next time. Don't get me wrong my sister-in law is dope and I see why Romelo married her, but the last thing I wanted to hear on a Saturday night is a sister nagging me.

Gina parted her lips to rant some more but Romelo cut her off, "Nah babe I got it. I know your tired of Gina preaching to you, but she has some valid points. For every woman you've fucked over there's a consequence waiting to happen. Cherish seems like a dope girl who genuinely cares for you unlike those other birds who's using you as their next come up. I know you're going to do whatever but let go of her now if you're not ready to do right. By the way let that be the first and last time you speak to my wife like that or you'll be picking up your jaw up off the floor."

Braxton and Kobe continued playing pool without me and pretended like they weren't listening. My brother pushed passed me, making himself comfortable in the recliner while Gina red lips formed into a smirk. I told you he was whipped.

Beep. Beep. **Nikki: Stop acting like you don't miss me.**

Some unexpected nudes blessed my brown eyes, making my dick hard. Receiving messages like this was pure temptation. It was halftime and the boys were betting on who was going to win the season opener between Charlotte Hornets verses Chicago Bulls.

Braxton and Romelo placed a $50 bet on the Bulls and Kobe was going for the Hornets. "Everybody's committed Ace, who are you betting money on?" Braxton inquired.

"Man, I'm going for either team. Here's $100 for the winning time," I casually threw some bills on the table. "I'm dipping out a little early tonight fellas. I have some busy to tend too."

I dapped the boys up before I headed towards the exit of the mancave. Within earshot I heard my brother say, "Don't fuck up a good thing." The roaring noise from the engine starting was cut short when an incoming call from Cherish ran across my information screen. I let her call go to voicemail deciding to give Nikki a call instead.

"Get prepared for me to tattoo my name in your ass, I'm headed your way." I made a mental note to call Cherish back as I thought about my brother's last words, "Don't fuck up a good thing."

Too bad that's exactly what I going to do as I killed the lights and locked the doors to my Audi, jogging up to Nikki's front door.

Chapter 10

Oh, What A Night

Cherish

It's officially GHOE! This past week has been a blur. I was up late catching up on work duties and maintaining my composure as Aaron started ghosting me again but this time his ass didn't have a reason to be distance. I had a good mind to call and cuss him out over his voicemail for the umpteenth time in four days, but I wasn't going to let the bullshit ruin my day.

I took half the day off from the work to start a much needed party weekends with my girls. I switched from my signature nude heels to a pair of Bohemian pearl tasseled sandals. I feathered my bang, outline my lips brown and finished with a clear coat of gloss giving off a semi-nude lip. I tried my hardest to get a full view of my appearance but having to rely on half a mirror was making this task difficult. Fuck it, my ass always looks great in clapper pants. If anything was out of place Tori would fix it.

I sported a multi-colored clapper set with the base color being gold with green, blue, green, red, and white stripes decorating the fabric. I pulled the bando top up a smidge to ensure no side boob was hanging out. I met Tori in parking garage across the street from Wells Fargo. My assistant was dressed to the nines in all-white pants with a rip at the knees and a slightly oversized white tee with red Steven Madden sandals. The way I was feeling and looking I was ready to act up for the day. I took a couple of pictures for the gram using the caption *that ass, that ass, that ass, that ass, she bad, she bad* for one of my backshot poses. I tagged him in the comments being petty, knowing he'll respond after seeing the pictures. Aaron better straight up before I bless one of these Greensboro men with my number.

"She ready!" I spoke with sass, waiting for the uber to pull up and drop us off less than two miles away. We were too cute to be mistaken as street walkers.

The bar crawl started at Fat Tuesday, where I order "Call A Cab", which is the strongest drink on the menu. "Cheers to a popping weekend!" Tori exclaimed after retrieving her drink. We tapped our cups together, started slurping down the drinks, and headed over to the lawn where the DJ was playing some early 2000's musically hits.

I was sipping on my fourth drink, a long island iced tea. Tori and I were posted up against a wall at Tranquilo, the last and final bar before the block party. I linked arms with Tori swaying from side to side embracing the culture as "Swag Surf" sounded through the building.

"Cherish your phone is ringing," Tori mentioned, taking notice of the flashing LED lights from my iPhone. I screened the caller ID feeling satisfied with seeing Aaron blowing up my phone. I ignored this call and the next two to teach him a lesson.

Ding. Ding. **Aaron: I know you're screening your calls. Don't keep showing your ass on the gram. I'm not with the petty games your trying to play.**

Me: Don't try to check me after you've been MIA for days. Last time I check this is my ass to show off to whomever and the way I'm feeling my ass is about to be riding another nigga.

"Damn Cee!", I thought to myself. I was certainly drunk because sober me would've written a paragraph instead of a quick clapback. I like Aaron and I'm lowkey obsessed with being in love again, but he needed to know early on I wasn't going to play another round of him ghosting me.

Two hours later, the block party was ending, and I was tired as fuck. My back ached from popping my ass too much, I felt sleepy as fuck from the all the alcohol, and my hair was getting poofy as hell from sweating. I felt and likely looked a mess. I waited for Tori to finish kicking it with a little friend she made before I searched for an uber.

"Girl today was lit beyond words, but a sister is tireddd," I spoke in my southern accent.

"Girl who you are telling, my new friend wants to link up later, but I think I'll have to pass until I feel rested up and rejuvenated."

The uber driver pulled into the parking garage and I couldn't be happier to head home and caught some zzzz's. "It's been real love, call or text me when you get home."

I told her "Goodbye," belted up and peeled out into the chaotic street, desiring to lay in bed with a quickness.

Kenly

Click clack, click clack, could be heard down the shallow staircase as my heels hit the concrete stairs. I strolled down to the second floor knocking on Cherish's door. Tonight, is going to be the start of an epic weekend.

"What up bitch! How was the bar crawl? Wait, why aren't you dressed yet?"

She sourly uttered, "The bar crawl was cool. Sorry, I forgot to text you and let you know I'm not going out tonight."

Umph typically Cherish, she can be a real moody bitch sometimes. All this week we've talked about getting lit this weekend and now she's acting funny. I rolled my eyes when she turned around to open the fridge.

"Come on sis. It's GHOE. Plus, this is your first-time experiencing homecoming, we're supposed to be living it up." I thought I sounded convincing but Cherish's resting bitch face said otherwise.

"I'm tired Ken, I had to work this morning and the bar crawl wore me out. It's not like you still wouldn't have a good time without me."

Inhale…exhale…inhale…exhale, was my brief breathing pattern to avoid an argument. Two of my homegirls I meet at work were going out with us tonight. Cherish isn't fond of the outside friends Brittish and I have made. She doesn't realize we enjoy her company, but nobody wants to deal with a moody friend all the time, hence the reason we had to make outside friends.

"Well, I understand you're not feeling up to it," I recited as I walked towards the door. Cherish quickly saw me out. I settled into my car remembering to say a prayer for a safe, but lit night as I burned rubber down the highway. Some scary shit always makes the news when GHOE occurs.

✳✳✳

My homegirls, Winnie, Winter, and I stood at the crossway of Washington Street and South Elm waiting for the traffic light to change. I bent over to pick up my lipgloss off the concrete when I heard a familiar laugh through the chaotic streets. Nah, I must be tripping.

We scurried to the other side when the traffic light signaled pedestrians had the right of way. My feet were starting to hurt already, I've should've worn a platform heel instead of these damn fuchsia stilettos. We had a couple more blocks to go before we'd reach Tranquilo.

I hear the familiar voice but this time it was accompanied with a snickering laugh. I wrecked my brain trying recall who's voice it was. I stopped midway of the sidewalk looking around to match a face with the voice, it was annoying that I couldn't make out who it was.

"Kenly, are you good? What's wrong boo?" Winnie questioned. Before I could respond Winter chimed in "Nah she's not good. Look who's approaching us to your right, the devil himself."

Low and behold I see Jaylen noncommitted ass nearing my perimeter with a basic redbone attached to his side. They look like happy lovebirds laughing and shit. I shook my head in disbelief, he's always been a clown, literately and figuratively.

I started to run and hide but what's the point. It's homecoming, he's an Aggie alumni meaning I was bound to run into him this weekend.

I stepped off the sidewalk into an empty outline for a parking space. "What's the game plan Ken?", Winnie and Winter asked in unison showing their twin telepathy. I contemplated for a second whether I should remain the old Kenly or try to be the bigger person this time.

"Hey, Jaylen it's funny running into you tonight." Nothing about this moment was funny but fuck it I'm attempting to be the bigger person by speaking.

"Oh shit, what up Ken" he stated with a surprised facial experience. "This is Kandi... my girlfriend."

Come again, I know this nigga didn't say girlfriend. I was ready to flip downtown Greensboro to uptown Greensboro the way anger circulated throughout my body. Jaylen's dumber than I thought.

I swept a piece of curly hair behind my ear, "Nice to meet you Kandi. He must have a thing for ladies with a K." The opportunity to be shady was too tempting to pass up.

Kandi gave him a "what she means" look and started firing off questions, exemplifying typical crazy female behavior. I tapped the twins letting them know it was time to go. I quickly threw in a "Have a good weekend" before we walked away.

Winnie gave me props for how I handled the situation, but I felt like shit on the inside. It's been less than a month since he was outside my car begging for another chance, now he's got a whole girlfriend. Ain't that a bitch!

I handed the bouncer my ID and waited for security to finish their search. Some low budget project chicks were cursing the host out and creating the perfect storm for a girl fight. Luckily security decided to check our tickets and we entered the bar that was giving off slight club vibes.

"BOTTOMS UP BITCHES!" Winnie exclaimed as we took our third shot of henny. The building was packed to capacity. Surprisingly it didn't smell like ass crack with everybody bouncing around and acting foolish the minute the DJ dropped Apeshit.

Winter and Winnie were walking around mingling while I choose to hold down our table. A couple of eligibility bachelors were in the building, but one guy caught my eye. He looked thug-life but something about his demeanor led me to believe it's more to his story. He wore a fitted white tee covered with a denim jacket and denim jeans, and red Air Jordan 11's. A gold Jesus piece dancing around his neck while he sported a close fade with ocean waves. Yeah, he was serving thug life vibes.

"Stop staring and go talk to him. You've never been shy, don't start acting brand new now," Winnie whispered in my ear.

"Bihh, you almost caught this two-piece sneaking up on me like that," I playfully joked. "I'm not acting shy. We've exchanged eye contact a few times but until he approached me I'm going to chill and sip my drink."

"Child please, let me help you out," was all she said before disappearing into the crowd. I scrolled through social media for a minute when Winnie came back with more than just a number.

"Jared this is my homegirl Kenly. Kenly this is Jared. Now we're all acquainted my work here is done." She made herself scarce once again.

"I caught you checking for me, with the flirty eyes. I was going to approach before the night over but your homegirl sped up my intentions," He spoke smoothly revealing his bottom grill.

I maintained my composure as if I wasn't interested, but on the inside, I was intrigued by his present.

Jared

Shawty was good girl who might wanna get down with the gangsters

Slim Thug lyrics ran through my mind as I'm listening to Kenly talk.

"I'm not trying to be up in your business but what do you do for a living?" she asked. This was a loaded question I wasn't prepared to answer. How do you tell somebody you work at bank but your moving weight and seeking revenge for your homeboy?

"It's been a long week at work but let's not talk about work tonight." I waved down one of the bottle girls ordering a beer for myself and lil' mama ordered a liquid marijuana.

We chopped it up for a good minute when Juvenile classic anthem "Back That Ass Up". I could tell shawty was a true twerker from the way she hopped up out of the seat. To my surprise nothing but booty graced my lap. She started throwing her ass back in a circular motion.

I squeezed her hips embracing the moment. Having a normal night out without running the streets with my GLOCK 17 on deck felt good. Lil' mama had no clue how much she was blessing me with this private lap dance.

Her vibe was dope, maybe she could be my next lady. She might be down to ride with me till the very end. I promised myself after I sell ten more bricks and murdered Malik's killer I was getting out of the game for good. I was pushing more coke to make sure Slim and her daughter would be good for while or at least until my business venture popped off.

I'm grateful to have my bank position as value proof of employment but the chump change I was making wasn't enough to survive. Good thing I saved up a big bank stash until my plan fell into place. I needed this plan to pan out soon. I'm popping mollies twice a day to keep with my double life. Then to top it off Roman mentioned the other day he was considering letting me take over the drug ring. The thought crossed my mind a few times but so far, I'm leaning towards the decision of saying "Nah." I had to give him a definite answer about learning the ropes within a few days. Whew a nigga was stressed and damn near stretched thin.

I brought my attention back to the show in front of me. Lil' mama was still doing her thing when I got a call from one of the coke fends, about a potential suspect. Ugh, duties call, times like this is exactly why I didn't want this lifestyle. I love the money, but I didn't want to stop whatever I was doing because the streets were calling me. I let Kenly finish her moment wishing I didn't have to departure so soon. She didn't seem mad and understood I had some things to take care of. I got her number promising to get up with later. I got the crew's attention, headed out on my next mission. The thought of blowing a nigga's brains out excited me.

Aaron

I stared at Cherish's Instagram feeling pissed all over again at the comments under her pictures. Yeah, I fucked Nikki and I'll probably fuck some more bitches before I completely commit to her, but she wasn't supposed to get a nigga back like that. Shawty told me she was different, but I took that shit for a joke.

"Braxton, I thought Winter was at some bar down Elm Street, I swear we've been walking for a little minute now. Maybe she should've called an Uber." Winter was Braxton's longtime girlfriend. We were enjoying a nagging free night from women at Shooter's Bar and Grill when Winter called needing a ride home saying she's too fucked up to drive.

"Mannn stop complaining. You've been an asshole tonight. What's shaking?"

"Cherish has me bent. She's pretty, educated, and everything in between but I don't know man. I've been ignoring her since I sampled some old pussy the other day, until she posted some thirst traps photos on the gram. I was livid, she supposed to be loyal no matter what."

"Ace, do you hear yourself? I try to stay out of your love affairs, but you can either be a hoe or care for one woman. Trying to do both is a disaster waiting to happen."

For the past few days I've been distanced from Cherish. After smashing up Nikki's insides I wasn't ready to lie to her face or even lie over the phone. Sometimes I wonder if I'm a sex addict and I hate to admit it, but maybe my brother was right about needing to let shawty go.

We walked a couple more blocks before we saw Winter and rest of the three live crew. They looked like they had a good night, too good of a night. Winter was sitting on the hood of somebody's car, Winnie was damn near passed out on the sidewalk, and some pretty vixen was chilling against the driver side.

"Braxtonnnn, I'm so glad to see you babeee," Winter slurred falling into Braxton's muscular arms and he motioned for me scoop up Winnie. I caught a glance at ole' girl when I walked pass to pick up Winnie, throwing her over my right shoulder. Shawty looked lit from her glassy eyes but sexy none the less with the plum hair and slim thick waist, but the twins on the other hand were bent to the point of no return. Winnie started pounding on my back with these baby hits not realizing I was eating those punches left and right. I was going to holla at lil' mama as she stood there looking bad as fuck, but Winnie was cock blocking with her rowdy ass behavior.

"Put me downnn…Ace" she pleaded but it was falling on deaf ears. Braxton checked in with the anonymous friend ensuring she was straight before we took off for this long ass walk to the car. The one thing I hate about GHOE is parking downtown is limited and the lot near Fat Tuesday's was the only space available this time of night.

"Wait...what's your name?" Lil' momma chimed in, diminishing her shy appearance. I did a 360 making official eye contact with her brown eyes.

"I'm Ace pretty thing." I extended my free hand out to her.

"I'm Kenly. I don't mean to be too forward, but I saw you looking at me. If you wanted my number all you had to do was ask." Shawty was confident and grasped my interest quickly. We exchanged numbers and said our goodbyes.

Half way to the car Winnie was passed out and Winter was resting easy with her head on Braxton's shoulder ridding his back and holding onto his neck for dear life. Between the chilly breeze and noisy downtown traffic, I'm wondering how the hell they fell asleep that quick.

Curiosity was getting the best of me, so I had to ask, "What do you know about Kenly?"

"Man, what did we talk about earlier. I'm not helping your ass hook with any more women. You were just pissed about shawty being on the gram but now you're on to the next chick. Figure out if you want that girl and stop making black brothers look bad. Shit it's niggas like you that give us brothers a bad rep."

"Damn, when did you become pussy whipped too. I expected this bullshit from my brother but not too long ago you were thotting right along with me."

"You're right Ace I'm pussy whipped like a mother fucker. I'm going to drop y'all asses off and go home to fuck the shit of my girl, but you on the other hand will likely be sleeping alone tonight. Thotting was cool but let me be the first to tell you loyal box triumphs some new pussy every time. You swear ole' girl is everything and more but like most niggas you continue to search for something better. Appreciate what you have before it becomes what you had."

As much as I wanted to be mad I knew Braxton was speaking straight facts. Maybe after GHOE I'll attempt to stop hoeing until then I'm a free man.

Chapter 11

The Calm Before the Storm

Kenly

Beep, beep, beep...I hit the snooze button on the alarm drifting back to sleep.

Tweet. Tweet. Fuck it, sleeping in was a no go this morning thanks to that damn phone. I rolled over grabbing my device to see I had a message from an unknown number.

336-545-7777: Good morning beautiful

"Oh, hell who could this be?" I thought to myself. I text back asking who it was before I put my phone on the charger. I ransacked my medicine cabinet for some Excedrin. I felt like my forehead was going to split open from the pounding headache I was experiencing.

I checked my phone just in time to see the nameless number belonged to Ace. Instantly, the memories of last night hit me like Tina did Ike in the limo. Damn, I had way too many drinks last night, feeling unsure how I got home safely.

I checked in with the twins hoping we were still going to the homecoming game. I headed into the bathroom to handle my hygiene, giving myself roughly an hour and a half to get ready for the game.

Beep. Beep. Beep. My phone was hotline bling this morning. Ace was keeping a steady conversation going and Jared just sent me a message. I patted myself on the back for successfully snagging two numbers, although Jared seemed a little rough around the edges.

I flipped the comforter back on my bed and sat on my all white bed bench to lace up my burgundy pumas. I took the steps two at time until I reached the bottom floor. I hit the unlock button as I neared my 2018 white Jaguar.

Parking at A&T was nuts which made my road rage be on ten. Finally, traffic was moving, and I whipped into the first open park I seen. Honk, honk. The loud horn saved me from walking into oncoming traffic. I took a pause from texting realizing nothing was worse worth becoming road kill.

I meet Winter and Winnie at the stadium entrance. We sat near the box office and had the perfect view of the Golden Delights famous p funk entrance. The band was magnificent, and the dancers were bound to pop their hip out of place from swaying and bucking. I tried to enjoy the game although I'm not a football fan, but the fall atmosphere and noisy crowd was everything. It's nearing halftime and I've half way been paying attention to the game. Ace and Jared were more holding my attention better then any football game would.

"Ken, get off that damn phone and watch the game. We went thru too much trying to finesse a ticket for you to be blowing us off." I locked my phone, feeling bad. My girl had a point because at the last minute I decided to go to the game, but it was already sold out. The twins bribed somebody near campus to surrender their ticket.

"Ugh, fine I'll put my phone away once the half time performance starts, you know the band was why I really stepped out today." The crowd went wild when the quarterback scored a touchdown making the score 21-14 giving the aggies the upper hand against Hampton University.

Tweet. Tweet. Another incoming message from Ace which was a picture this time. I prepared myself to see a dick print pic, but I was happily surprised to see a funny meme about homecoming.

ME: LOL! Love this one.

Aaron: So, where do you work at?

Me: I'm a chemist at Carolina liquid chemistries. I'm a science nerd. What about you?

Aaron: Oh shit, you're a little scientist on the low but I'm the CEO of my own trucking company. You should look it up, it's called Ross Trucking Company

Holy shit! Faint flash backs from last night made my hands clammy. There's no way in hell Ace could be Aaron.

"Girl, why do you look like you saw a ghost?" Winter questioned. I attempted to explain myself, but the chaotic crowd made that near to impossible. I whispered in Winter's ear and she transferred the message to Winnie before they followed me down the blenchers. I needed somebody to help me rationalize the craziness I was coming to terms with.

"What's the issue boo? That's Braxton's homeboy, he's cool people," Winter said. She gave me the clear-cut run down on Ace who I'm presuming to be Aaron. From the sound of the things he's the exact person Cherish is dating.

"The issue is I think this is Cherish's babe. Oh my god y'all was I that fucked up that I couldn't recognize his face. Shit why would this happen to me? I swear I've got to stop drinking," I ranted away like a crazy black woman.

"Chill Ken! You don't know if it's him yet your making assumptions. I couldn't tell you how fucked up you were seeing as I was too far gone myself. Just tell Cherish everything that happened and see if it's the same nigga. He might have a twin running around town, but if it is him he's no good anyways."

I rubbed my temples hoping to relieve the amount of stress I was encountering. "Winnie we both know this is the same man and you don't know Cherish like I do. How do I look my best friend in the face and tell her the guy she's crazy about is another trifling no good nigga? Then tell her I know this information because I somewhat started talking to him briefly. I don't know about you, but I'd be pretty pissed if someone in my circle came to me with this shit."

The twins debated back and forth how I should handle the situation but none of their suggestions were worth a damn. I needed to talk to somebody who knew Cherish the way that I do to seek some advice. Hmm...who's better to call then Brittish. She knows Cherish and I better than we know ourselves sometimes.

I ditched the twins and left the game during the third quarter. I no longer was in the mood for people and couldn't think straight with this situation throbbing in my dome. My blue tooth connected soon after Siri called my Ace Boone Coon aka Brittish. I filled her in on last night events and today's current revelations. Telling the story for the second time wasn't so bad maybe Cherish will feel the same when I talk to her.

Brittish let out a deep sigh, "I just pulled up his profile on the company website and that's him. You already know what you need to do, you have to tell her. You have to tell her NOW, TODAY! Cherish will be hurt but she'll know you didn't do this to be malicious."

I closed my eyes, taking a moment to breathe and woosah. "I'm going to tell her Brit. Sometime today I'll tell her. Let's pray she understands."

I stopped responding to Ace, knowing I had no choice but to crush my best friend's feelings.

Cherish

I woke up feeling shitty. My throat was sore, and I felt like I was running a fever. I took my temperature looking at the thermometer, I was running a low-grade fever of 99.2. Umph so much for having a productive day. I went to lay in my heaven-sent bed, between the memory form mattress and cooling gel pillows I felt like I was sleeping on a cloud nine.

I checked my phone in between naps getting pissed off again. I haven't heard from Aaron in two days ago. Ugh why did I entertain his ass. I'm too grown to be playing petty game with a nigga. I swear the next time I see or talk to him he's going to feel my wrath.

I had enough of napping when I fluffed the pillows, sitting up in bed scrolling through the gram. The Shaderoom comments had me dying with the what would you text back scenario. I should send in a screenshot of Aaron's message to see what other people would text back, I thought briefly. Nah I going to let this nigga take me to that level of pettiness.

One of my ratchet television shows played in the background when I heard knock, knock. Lord who the fuck is disturbing my peaceful pajama day. I slipped on a robe, peeking through the peek hole feeling unhappy to see Kenly. I wasn't in the mood for company, but I unlocked the door and let her come in anyways.

"Hey girl, how are you doing? No shade but you look a mess sis."

"Girl I think I'm coming down with a bad cold. How has your weekend?" I plopped down on the couch, kicking my feet up on the ottoman.

"It was cool, I met some new people but other than that it was a typically packed night at the bar. Same old same old, bitches and niggas flexing and hella of a lot of twerking was going on."

"I'm glad you had a great time with Winter and Winnie. I'm sorry if I came off as rude Friday night, you know how I get when I don't want to be bothered with people."

"Of course, I understand, you've never been a fan of hanging with the crowd, but how was your weekend?"

"Girl it was chill. I didn't do nothing outside of the bar crawl. I decided to travel to Raleigh to spend time with my godmother."

"That sounds fun, but girl I have to tell you something."

I let out a sigh preparing myself for the worst. "Girl what is it? I can't take no more bad news right now. This past week has been eventful." My life was a wreck when Dame left, and to fill the void I drowned myself in work until Aaron showed up and showed the fuck out being a much need distracted. Ugh I see why I stopped fucking with these niggas. All they're good for is creating problems. I was better off being focus on my career.

"What's going on boo?" Kenly seemed concerned, but I left her question unanswered. "I don't know what's going on but I'm here for you. I wish you would stop holding everything in."

I rolled my eyes, I believed in telling people things on a need to know bases. If I didn't tell somebody something clearly, I felt like they didn't need to know now. People are bit too nosy for me including my best friend. She means well but I'll talk about my things when I'm good and ready. I stared out the window to avoid looking at Kenly.

"Well I can't make you talk to me. I'm going to head out and I hope you feel better. By the way I'm cooking four cheese pasta tonight, your welcome to grab a plate. Love you girly."

I told her thanks and locked the door behind her. I checked the time on the stove, it's 2pm which means I'm taking another nap before I attempt to do some stuff for work.

***

I wiped the sleep out of eyes taking a bizarre look around the room. The TV was blasting, and the dark atmosphere meant I slept until nightfall. Geeze, this fever was draining my energy. "Whewww," I sounded letting out a deep ass yawn.

I rumbled through my top drawer to find a t-shirt to cover the sports bra I was wearing before I went to Kenly's apartment. I'm grateful she was cooking because I was in no mood to have the stove rocking at 8 o'clock at night. Maybe if I ate something I'd feel better.

"I didn't think I was going to see you tonight. I figured you would continue to habitant for rest of the day, but come on in."

"Yeah yeah, whatever. You know food is the one thing I'll get out of bed for."

I walked into the kitchen to fix myself a to go plate when I noticed the bar area was set up with two plates and glasses. Here Kenly was trying to be a good friend, making sure I'm straight before she starts her romance evening. Curiosity had me wondering who she was entertaining, but anybody was better than Jaylen.

"Sorry for being a bitch I'm grateful for the food. I'm too lazy to cook or order some food." I gave her a hug and reached for the door handle.

"You have it smelling good in here", a deep male voice commented. Curiosity got the best of me, so I turned around and saw Jared. Jared, from the bank interview. Jared who resembled J. Cole. What the fuck?

"Hey Mr. Daniels." An awkward silence filled the air

"Hey...Ms. Wright" he stumbled out.

Kenly was confused, "Wait y'all know each other?"

"Well yeah I guess you can say we know each other. You remember when I told you I meet a cutie who reminded me of J. Cole. Well this is him."

Mixed emotions overcame me. I wasn't mad or at least I didn't think I was, but I was shocked to see him kicking it with Kenly. I mean I was about to go on a date with him. I rushed out the door before anything else was said. The last time I seen him things ended on a sour note and I was in no mood to rehash the past especially when I'm unsure where I stand with Aaron.

I locked myself in for the night and settled back into bed. I sound like a couch potato because I am one. I love laying in the bed more than I liked sitting in my expensive ass living room. I spent damn near $1500 decking out the living out to only spend majority of my time in the bed.

I ate most of my food, but my mind was bogged with what just happened. I had to call Brittish and fill her in. She went on a couple's trip during the worst time and was expected to be back in town today. I hope she has time to listen for a minute.

Brittish answered the phone rambling on and on about her weekend getaway to Cali. It was good to know everybody man wasn't showing their asses, but I was happy when she finished talking so we could get down to the real matter at hand.

"Britt I'm glad you had a lit weekend, but shit has gone haywire. Aaron is acting funny and I'm 2.5 seconds from cutting his ass off. Then Kenly is seeing Jared the guy I told you guys about a few weeks ago. Girl shit is crazy." I ranted on and on about Aaron and Jared.

"Woah, slow down. I half hear everything you just said, let's break things down. First off I'm glad Kenly told everything I was scared for minute that you'd be mad." Hmm...what was she was talking about Kenly hasn't told me anything.

"Wait Kenly hasn't told me nothing. Spill it now! I hate secrets and I really hate y'all both know some shit that I don't know!"

"Umm...I'm going to let Kenly tell you this news... you need to hear it from her," Brittish stated slowly.

"Somethings up and I suggest you start talking now. If you're really my best friend, you'll tell me." Pulling the best friend card always gets Brittish to tell the truth.

"Well. Um. I don't know how to say this, but Kenly meet and exchanged numbers with two guys Friday night. As you probably figured one of the guys was Jared and the other guy was...Aaron. She told me she was tipsy and didn't realize it was him until the next day. Please don't flip shit!"

My heart dropped, did Britt just say what I think she said. "Wait what. Stop play Brittish… did just say Aaron's name?" I felt my blood pressure sky rocking from the heat radiating through my body.

"Cherish I'm sorry. I was under the impression she was going to tell you everything. I'm not sure what happened but let her explain—"

I ended the call before Brittish could finish defending Kenly's snake ass. So, Kenly is talking to Jared and Aaron. Why the fuck would she do that? I'm not mad about Jared but Aaron was a different story. So, I'm home feeling terrible and they're out mingling and shit. Oh so Aaron acting single single. Wow this was turning into the night from hell. I had to get to the bottom of this news dropping information, starting with Aaron's trifling ass.

I facetimed him but no answer. I called him for the fifth time before he answered my call.

"Why are you blowing up my phone? I thought you were single and serving ass to somebody else." His smart ass had some nerve trying to check me.

I turned the TV off and paced the floor. "You got some nerve trying to check me but you're out here talking to other bitches. Just tell me if you got a girls number this weekend?"

"Look I have female friends and I mean yeah I got some numbers but why does it matter?" The fuck does he mean he has female friends.

"Wow so this whole time you've been begging me to be yours you've been doing you. I can't believe this shit. So, what was your point in bothering me? Matter fact don't even answer that. I just need to know if one of the numbers you got was from a girl named Kenly, she's slim thick with plum colored hair."

"Wait let me check my phone." I could hear him tapping in my ear. "Yeah one of them were named Kenly," he said coolly. Tears streamed from my eyes and my heart dropped into my stomach.

"Aaronnn, Kenly is my best friend nigga. So, have you seen her since Friday? Have y'all kissed? I need details."

He gave me his version of Friday night saying she asked him for his number but for all I know his ass could be lying. The upside was nothing more than text messages and some inappropriate pictures had taken place. I hung up on him too after I got my questions answered. I knew deep down inside something about him didn't sit well with me. Who would've thought he'd be a player who coincidentally started talking to my best friend. Wow, Greensboro is a small world.

I fell out on the floor crying my eyes out to the point where they were swelling, and I had a headache. I haven't felt this kind of pain since Dame boarded American Airlines a year and a half ago. I peeled myself off the brown fuzzy carpet, wiping my tear stained face. My emotions went from being hurt to angry. I wanted to fight, beat somebody's ass, destroy some shit. I needed an outlet. My mind was spinning out of control when I decided to go on an ass whooping tour. I didn't care how bad I was feeling and I damn sure no longer care about the good girl imagine anymore. I'm tired of people fucking me over and thinking shit was sweet. The Memphis side of me was popping out tonight.

I laced up my all black Roshoe and took the stairs two at a time to get to Kenly's place. It didn't take her long to open the door. I thought about letting her explain herself, but I got so mad I ended up punching her in the jaw.

"What the hell Cherish?" She rubbed her left jaw to comfort the pain she was feeling.

"Don't play stupid. Brittish told me everything and Aaron confirmed the story. You really set out to get Aaron's number. You're a conniving little bitch!" I tried to hit her again, but she blocked my blow this time.

"Listen that's not the whole story. I didn't know it was Aaron until the next day. I was tipsy, it was dark outside, I couldn't tell it was him until he mentioned where he worked. I swear Cherish nothing more happened than texting for a couple of hours happened before I ended the situation. I was going to tell you. I promise Cherish I was going to tell you. How was I supposed to look you in the face and tell you Aaron is doing his own thing?"

The nerve of this bitch to start crying, as if I was in a sympathetic mood tonight. Fuck NO! Just the sight of her disloyal ass made me charge at her again, successfully knocking her to the floor. I rained blows on her pretty caramel face, but she wasn't a punk, she got some licks in too. Jared made his present known again when he pulled me off her.

"You're supposed to be my best friend, my best fucking friend! Why didn't you just tell me? I'm looking like a fool taking this nigga serious. Out of all people you could've talked that night why did both people turn out to be people I'm familiar with." I wrestled away from Jared . There was no sense in hitting her pathetic ass again, it wasn't worth it. Loyalty means everything, but I guess expecting loyalty from some people was asking for too much.

Brittish and Aaron kept calling me to the point where I turned my phone off for the night. I turned on the shower, hopping in once the water was scorching hot. The water soothed me as a river of tears started to fall yet again.

Brittish

The famous Contagious talking scenario "Oh it's about to be my shit" keep replaying in my mind. Cherish refused to pick up my phone calls and Kenly wasn't answering the phone either.

"Babe, I should go over there. I know my girls' things are getting ugly. They already have a love hate relationship, but this bullshit here may end things for good."

Grant responded thru the receiver, "No you're staying your ass at home. Cherish and Kenly are grown regardless of what happens you can't save their friendship. They need to figure things out on their own. If it's meant for them to be friends they'll survive this moment." I could always count on Grant to be the voice of reason.

I walked into my walk-in closet to pick out something to wear to work tomorrow. I searched through the hangers and pulled out a few options. My phone started vibrating in my housecoat pocket. Although I was planning to mind my business I was glad to see Kenly was calling me back.

"Sis what's going on? I've been trying to get in touch with you. I accidentally spilled the beans to Cherish. I'm so sorry. I thought you told her everything after we talked yesterday. For real love I'm sorry."

"Save it Britt. You've ruined my friendship. Cherish is beyond pissed. She came up here and left me with a black eye, but that's beside the point. How did you accidentally tell her? Make that make sense Britt."

Shit, now I really feel bad. I figured Cherish would be in her feelings but hearing a physical altercation took place was shocking. Yeah Kenly may have a point, their friendship might be a done deal after that.

"Listen she called me to talk about Aaron and mentioned Jared's name. I was half listening while she rambled on about Aaron so naturally I assumed you told her everything. I promise I didn't tell her to be messy. I feel bad. Just give her some time she'll eventually understand this was a big mix up."

"Tuh... who are you kidding Britt? She's done with me and quick frankly I'm done with you. If you would've given me a chance to tell her and explain myself, she wouldn't have gone apeshit. Thank you so much for ruining my friendship," she stated in a sarcastic tone.

"You know what, I'm not doing this with you. You were the one who was too fucked up to realize that was Aaron. You were the one who chose not to tell her right away. I'll admit I didn't do this to be messy, but you need to take responsibility for your behavior and bad choices. Maybe you're the one who needs to stop drinking."

"Whatever hoe!" She shouted into the phone then hung up. This bitch had the audacity to call me a hoe yet I'm the one who's rocking a ring. Umph, if one more person hung on me I was going to spaz. I started to call Grant again, but I dialed Dash's number instead she's always in the mood to hear the latest gossip.

Chapter 12

The aftermath

Cherish

"Morning Tori. I need you to clear my schedule for the day. I'm only here for a half a day, then I'm going home."

I walked away from the desk not caring if she responded back or not. I unlocked my door, started up the computer system, and decided not to finish the rest of my morning routine. I needed something stronger than coffee to cope with life, but drinking at nine a.m. wasn't a good choice.

I put my head down on the desk since the computer was doing an update. My emotions and mental state continued to be on ten, and no matter how many Ibuprofens I took, I had a migraine for days.

I lifted my head up when I heard my office door open. Out of all the times I've told Tori to just walk right in, she picked the worst day possible to take me seriously.

"Boss lady, what's going on? Talk to me, and don't say nothing is wrong. You look a mess and seemed upset when you walked in."

I blew my breath in the air, preparing to share this awful story yet again. By the end of reliving the night from hell, I was crying again.

"I'm a loving and caring individual, Tori. Why would they do me like this?" I felt like I was searching for answers that neither party had for me. Kenly's worst excuse was she was tipsy, and the lightening outside was dark. Then, Aaron's weak ass commentary was to blame everything on Kenly. Maybe those two reckless motherfuckers belonged with each other.

Tori listened to me rant and comforted me whenever I broke down crying again. I know some people don't think this situation was that deep, but to me, it was. If you can't trust the people in your circle, who can you trust, which was the magical question I no longer had the answer to.

Kenly

I grabbed my Tarte mermaid foundation brush covering up the purple bruise under my eye. Cherish nicked my ass good. I honestly didn't care that she violated me if it meant we'd remain friends.

It's been a few days since everything popped off, and outside of Jared, I isolated myself from everybody. I'm good on Brittish, and Cherish has blocked my number. It may seem fucked up how much I'm communicating with Jared but falling out with two friends all at once did a number on me. I needed somebody, and for now, that somebody happens to be Jared.

I was riding to work bumping the latest Travis Scott album "Astroworld". Out of the blue, I had an incoming call from Lena, Cherish's mother. *I hope everything is okay,* I thought to myself before I answered the call. It was delightful to hear her warm voice. I love her momma as if she was my own, but it's too bad the days of us feeling like family were over. Her momma was a sweetheart for giving me a call even though her daughter hated me now. Talking to her mother created unwanted tears, and thankfully, Mrs. Wright comforted me. I reached for a napkin out of the glove compartment when I stopped at a red stoplight. I dabbed the tears from my face doing my best to not remove the makeup under my eye.

Despite her uplifting words, we both know Cherish doesn't forgive easily, and she damn sure don't plan on forgetting shit. I pondered on it over the last few days, beating myself up for my lack of good choices. I made a mental note to chillout with the drinks. I've criticized Brittish in the past for drinking, yet one of the worst things I've played a part in happened because I was drinking.

I turned my phone off once I stepped on the grounds of Carolina Liquid Chemistries. I should send a defected chemistry analyzer to Lab Corps to fuck up Brittish's DNA results. The thought of getting even with this broad is too tempting.

7 hours later

I was glad to be going home for the day, work felt mad long. On my way home, I thought of Cherish again. I stopped by Walgreens to find a card to express how sorry I was. I found the perfect card in the Hallmark section entitled "Tough Cookie." Indeed, Cherish was just that, a tough cookie who was mixed with sweetness and strength, hardly crumbled under pressure, and took life by the horns without asking for much support.

I wrote a personal message inside the card:

No matter how things may play out between us, I wanted you to know I'm sincerely sorry. I would never intentionally hurt you. For what it's worth, I blocked and deleted his number.

I know nothing can take your pain away but at least you see what type of man he was, and as you already know, you deserve better.

Take all the time you need to heal. I love you, and I'll never forget the imprint you've made on my life.

I left the card and her favorite bottle of wine, pink Moscato, at front door. I've done all I can do, now I have to wait and wonder when she's going to be in a forgiving mood.

Aaron

"I need a table for two please." I made a request with the young lady hosting at Olive Garden. A nigga was stressed between Cherish going off on me every other day and handling work business. The wait was brief with the host sitting me in the bar area.

"Long time no see, Aaron. The last thing I recall is being verbally kicked out of your apartment."

"Thanks for coming, sweetheart. I'm sorry about that, that's why I invited you to dinner. Have a seat." We took some time to look through the menu, ordering drinks and entrees shortly after.

"Listen, a lot has happened. I met somebody, she was incredible, but I fucked up. She's not going to take me back--"

Trina threw her hand in the air motioning for me to stop talking. "Did you really bring me here to talk about another bitch and think I would still want your no-good ass back?"

"Nah man, let me finish. I brought you here to say I'm sorry. I'm sorry for treating you bad and using you at my own expense. I don't want to be with you romantically, but I wanted to right my wrongs with all the women I've hurt including you, so there you have it. I'm truly sorry."

Trina's frown developed into a slight smile. My brother and homeboys tried to warn me against having my cake and eating it too. I've hurt plenty of women, but the damage I did to Cherish was a wakeup call. I'm going to do everything I can to win her back because she was a real one, and out of all the women I've fucked with, none of them could compare to her.

"Thank you for the apology. I never thought I'd get closure from you. I'm happy you're trying to change. Aaron, you have the potential to be a great man, but women aren't play toys. If you care for this girl the way you say you do, you have to do better. By better I don't mean flashing your money, you need to change your behavior. Go above and beyond with apologizing and give her all the time in the world to take you back. You're used to having women at your beck and call, but from the look of things, she's not that type."

I accepted Trina's word knowing she was speaking from the heart.

We caught up for a bit, and I invited her to the company's celebration event which was rapidly approaching. I swallowed the rest of my beer before I waved the waiter down for the check.

The restaurant was booming for a Thursday night with traffic constantly coming in and out the wooden double doors. I thought my eyes were deceiving me when I saw her stroll through the door. She looked flustered but sexy as hell in a black matching set with the words PINK in gold bling. I'm glad I spotted her before she noticed me giving me time to come up with a game plan to approach her. I wasn't trying to create a World Star moment after I spoke to her.

She must have tunnel vision seeing as she walked up to the bar and didn't notice I was sitting to the far left at the last table against the wooden panel. I dismissed myself from the table just in time to walk up to the bar and pay for her meal.

"I got it, bartender." I pulled out my bank card to take care of the bill.

She turned around gracing me with her face and presence. "Wow, you're stalking me now? If you know what's good for you, you'd get the hell out of my face."

She signed the receipt, grabbed her food, and attempted to walk away.

"Wait, hear me out. I've listened to you cuss me out and make assumptions, but I just want you to listen for a second," I pleaded with her. After putting up with her emotional unstable behavior this week, I deserved a chance to say something.

"Listen! Listen! Listen! You've got to be kidding me. I'm the last one who's going to listen to a damn thing you have to say. If you want to live to see tomorrow, I'd suggest you move out of my way."

The bar area fell silent with most people turning around in their seats to look at us. She tried to walk around me, but I blocked her every move. Olive Garden wasn't the place to have a standoff, but if I let her walk away again, she'd probably be gone forever.

Trina came back from the bathroom asking me what was going on before she went back to the back table.

"Who the fuck is this? Is this your new bitch?" Cherish spoke loudly. Baby girl was tweaking for real. I've never heard her say such foul words until this situation happened. *So much for not creating a scene,* I thought to myself.

"Calm down. Her name is Trina, but she's not my girl. I'm not going to lie to you, I used to mess around with her, but that's in the past. I know I messed up, but your homegirl asked for my number, not the other way around. If you want to be mad at anybody, you need to direct that energy towards her." She looked at me with an expression that read she was over it. I continued to talk and plead my case anyways until a glob of slimy residue hit my cheek. This bitch was really on one to spit in my face with such calmness and no remorse. Before I could rough up her ass up for pulling them childish antics the restaurant manager walked up to diffuse the situation.

"Excuse, me I don't know what's going on, but I suggest you guys leave before the police is called. You're disturbing our guests."

"I'm trying to leave, sir, but his bitch ass won't let me." I wiped the glob of spit from my face. My jaw started to flex, and my nose flared up. If she wasn't a female I cared for, she'd be picking herself up from the floor for the disrespectful shit she was pulling.

Trina walked up and whispered in my ear, trying to remind me how I was supposed to be showing Cherish I'm a changed man. I swear I wanted to change for her, lord knows I do, but she was pushing my patience to the point of no return with her antics. Change isn't an overnight process. I've been a fuckboy most of my life; transitioning to an understanding respectful gentleman was one hell of a task.

I took the manager's advice, stepping to the side letting her walk away before somebody called the police. With this huge advancement occurring for the trucking company, I couldn't afford to catch a charge.

I paid for our meals and left out the restaurant portraying the unfortunate image of an angry black man. As much as I care for Cherish, maybe the damage I've done is too significant to repair.

Chapter 13

Messy Messy

Brittish

"Babe, what time are you coming over tonight? I was going to order take out and suggest we watch season two of Marlon on Netflix." I never knew Marlon Wayans was funny until we started watching his TV show.

"Sounds like a plan, baby, but I have some errands to run this afternoon, then I'll be on my way." I started to drill him with questions, however I didn't want to come off as insecure. For a while now, I've found myself doing insecure shit such as checking his social media or popping up at his job once a week.

I wondered why I was marrying somebody I no longer trusted. To keep my mind from overthinking, I took out the cleaning supplies and started cleaning up my living room. I was moving my MacBook Air from the couch to the kitchen table when a crazy idea popped into my head. I contemplated if following his location was taking my insecurities too far.

Fuck it, I'm tired of wondering what he was up to and feeling like he's being secretive. I sat down pulling up his iCloud information, thank God I remembered his passwords. I texted my sister telling her to get ready to do a pop up on Grant. Normally, I would call one of my homegirls, but tension remained between the fab three. Cherish was still struggling with everything, and I refused to speak to Kenly until she apologized. I didn't need their issues interfering with my mission.

I drove in my parents' driveway, honking the horn for Dash. She came out the side door wearing a black adidas fit. She looked prepared to smoke somebody instead of handling a simple pop up.

"Dash, what's with the black fit? I told you we're going to do a pop up not going to war with Grant. I mean, I appreciate you being down to ride, but let's hope Grant isn't doing nothing stupid."

"I gotcha, sis. Where are we headed?"

"We're going to a location in the New Garden area. I've been watching his location and he's been at this address for over an hour. I Googled it and pulled up a house. I swear to God if he's messing around on me, this engagement is cancelled."

I drove past the house seeing two cars in the driveway recognizing Grant's Range Rover. I parked a few houses down running down the mission with Dash one more time.

I held my hand over the peep hole before I rang the doorbell. To my dismay, a pretty, petite, light-skinned lady was on the other side of the door. I needed more evidence before I lost my cool.

"Hello, are you here to view the house? I didn't think I booked anymore appointments for the day." Oh, so he's messing with a realtor and creeping on me at one of her housing properties? I wondered if she knew he was engaged.

"Um, I'm kind of here to see the house, but then again, I'm kind of here to see if Grant Taylor is in the area." Dash made her rounds around the house like we discussed on the way here.

"Well, I'm not able to answer questions about other clients, but I'd be happy to schedule an appointment to show you the house sometime tomorrow." She was trying to get rid of me, but I wasn't leaving until I saw Grant. Regardless if she knew about me, I wasn't going to fight her, but I damn sure was going to light Grant's ass up.

"Sweetie, let me give you the real tea. I'm engaged to a man named Grant, and it's highly important you reveal his whereabouts. I know he's somewhere in the area because his truck is outside. I'm not going to hit you, but I'm not leaving until I find him."

She pulled out her phone and dialed a number, I'm guessing she was calling him. She didn't refuse or make an argument leading me to believe she was scared shitless. Female to female, she could sense I wasn't here to play games.

"Hey, I'm not trying to rush you, but can you meet me in the foyer? I need to show you the built-in sound system."

Dash came back down the stairs with no incriminating information, and my nerves were on ten as we waited to see his lying ass. I couldn't wait to see how he was going to react when he saw me.

He cut the corner of the foyer looking giddy until he made eye contact with me.

"Hey Brittish, what are you doing here?" he spoke nervously.

"I should be asking you the same thing. You've been acting secretive, having all these errands to run suddenly, and somehow, you're alone with another female. Please explain yourself before I start acting ignorant."

Grant let out a sigh breaking the tension. "Brittish, it's not what you think. I already told you, I'm not cheating on you. Kendra is a realtor. If you would've trusted me a little while longer, I was going to tell you next week that I bought us a house. All the phone calls and errands were from meeting with Kendra to find the perfect house. I didn't plan to tell you like this, but surprise! This is your house if you'll accept it."

I felt so stupid. "Sis, I told you he wasn't cheating. You should listen to me more often." Dash chimed in. I gave her a look letting her know to be quiet.

"Whattt! You're not cheating. You bought a house, our first house." I placed my hand over my heart making sure I was alive and not dreaming. A few tears boarded my eyelids, my fiancé continued to amaze me. I walked over to him placing a kiss on his soft lips.

He pulled me in for a hug. "I love you ,babe, and I know you're serious about waiting until the nuptials before we officially live together. However, you can go ahead and move in next week after I sign the papers, and I'll move in after the wedding."

"Baby, I'm speechless. You're so thoughtful. I swear I'm done with the insecure bullshit. I haven't seen much of the house, but I can tell I'm going to love it. I don't want to move in with you, so despite my past feelings, I want us to move in together. I mean, we're always staying the night with each other anyways. I was afraid if we moved in together, we'd be another couple with a prolonged engagement. The fact you brought us a house reassures me we're in this for the long haul. I love you, baby!"

Dash and the realtor watched us have a heartfelt moment like we were in a classic 90's romance movie. My suspicions were finally put to rest. Kendra left the paperwork and gave us some privacy for Grant to show me and Dash around our new home.

My baby did his thing this time. The house was a four bedroom with four bathrooms, a deck with an inground pool, and a humongous walk in closet.

I have the ring, my king, and a new house. Before I know it, I'll be ready to pop out some babies.

Dame

I was relieved to make it back to the states after an eleven-hour plane ride, hustling through customs, and catching a connecting flight to Greensboro. I was willing to do some extreme shit to get my baby back. It took me a few weeks to get things situated, but I made it happen.

I secured a rental car since I was going to be in the states for a while. I lied to my coach in Italy telling him one of my family members was terminally ill, and I needed to come home for a while. He expressed his sympathy, deciding to approve my leave request. Pulling a bold move like this was putting everything on the line. Technically my contract might end after this year, or I could be traded during mid-season since I'm missing games that aren't related to an injury. At this point, I was ready to say fuck the contract anyways. I missed my family, Cherish, and basically my American lifestyle. Italy was cool, but what's the point of making money and being successful if it came without the other qualities of life?

I checked into my king size suit at the Sheraton hotel. I called my momma confirming I'd arrived in North Carolina, but I had some business to handle before I touched down in Charlotte. I took a shower, ordered room service, and verified Cherish's address with the private investigator. Brittish thought ending all contact with me meant I couldn't keep up with Cherish, but baby girl was dead wrong. I hired an investigator a few weeks back to keep tabs on her and making sure things between her and the fuckboy from IG weren't getting too serious. The latest update I got from the investigator revealed she wasn't rocking with him no more which was music to my ears.

I cruised around the city stopping at the mall to cop the new Jordan's. A couple of people recognized me and wanted to take some pictures. It was cool being a C list celebrity but wasn't the best idea to go to the mall, if I wanted to stay lowkey until I surprised Cherish.

I went to Edible Arrangements and ordered a strawberry and pineapple basket to be delivered to her job. Cherish is obsessed with eating fruits and being healthy. I remember her juices tasting sweet and that pussy getting super wet for me. I bit my bottom lip as flash backs of the good times resurfaced.

The day flew by quick with the clock on the dashboard reading seven p.m. I got off on exit 214 to get to her apartment. I parked beside her IS 250 Lexus being relieved she was home already on a Friday night.

I prayed to God almighty the moment I've thought about for quite some time was worth the wait.

"Here goes nothing." I knocked on the apartment door of unit C.

Cherish

I struggled to get in my apartment with my hands being filled with an edible arrangement and holding my cell phone to my ear while I talked to Brittish.

It'd been two weeks since my life fell to shambles, and for the first time in a while, I was feeling happy. I went to visit Brittish's new house during my lunch break, and some mysterious person sent me my favorite fruits. I hope this wasn't Aaron doing it this time. I'm done with him and Kenly. It's cute how they were still sending gifts as some type of peace offering. I must admit I've eaten every chocolate covered strawberry basket and sweet treats Aaron has sent to my job, and I thoroughly enjoyed the pink Moscato Kenly left at my door. I was angry, but I wasn't foolish enough to not entertain the treats they sent.

Then they were blowing up my phone for a while until I blocked them. If I didn't know any better, I would say they were still communicating because they were using the same tactics to get back in my good graces. No matter what they did once I said fuck you, I meant it.

"Girl, I'm in the house, I'll call you later, boo." I hung up the phone, sat the fruit basket on the counter, and started to unwind for the day. I switched from my casual Friday look into a red nightgown from PINK. It's safe to say I spend too much time at that store. I poured myself a glass of red Moscato, picked off a few pieces of fruit, and got comfortable on the couch to catch up on my TV shows.

Midway through an episode of Married to Medicine, there was knock at my door. *Who's stopping by unannounced?* Everybody knows to call before you drop by.

I swear my eyes were playing tricks on me. It looked like Dame was at my door when I peeped through the peephole. I undid the locks opening the door slowly unsure if I wanted to know if it was him.

Oh, my God! It's him, the ex-love of my life. I was in a state of shock. I hadn't seen or talked to him in almost a year and a half, yet he's standing at my door step. Just when I was trying to get my life back on track, here he comes resurfacing from the past. I'm not sure why he's here, but I'm pretty sure whatever the reason is was going to be some bullshit.

I held my door wide open letting the fall breeze send chills down my chocolate legs.

"Hello, Cherish. It's so good to see you again." I blinked my eyelids repeatedly remaining speechless. I even slammed the door and opened it again to make sure this moment was happening and not a dream.

"I know this is a shocker and really out of the blue, but I miss you, and I hate how things ended between us."

He gave me a sympathetic look with his endearing greenish eyes. I looked away not wanting to get memorized and pulled back into the hold he has on my heart.

"Dame, I used to pray for the day we would see each other again. I never thought about how I would feel if this day ever happened, and right now, I don't know how to feel. A part of me is happy, and the other part is angry."

"You're entitled to your feelings, love. Can I come in, or I'm asking for too much?" I stepped aside to let him in.

"How did you find me in Greensboro?" I had so many questions and things I needed to say.

"Don't judge me for this, but I hired a private investigator. I had an ole' friend keeping tabs on you, but they refused to help me anymore, leaving me no choice but to hire an investigator."

"Wow, with the right amount of money you can do whatever you want including paying somebody to unknowingly spy on me, but why now? What inspired you to come back after being gone all this time?"

"Truthfully Cherish, I always planned to come back for you, but seeing you on Instagram and hearing from Brittish how happy you were, I couldn't let somebody else come in and take my place."

My blood pressure was rising yet again as more secrets were revealed. It's bad enough Kenly briefly talked to Aaron and failed to tell me everything. Now Brittish has been communicating with Dame, and his selfish ass came back to make sure I didn't end up happy without him. Ain't this some shit.

"Dame…you sound selfish as hell. After all this time, your motive to come back to the states was to ruin whatever happiness I found in somebody after you left me and said, "I don't know what this means for us". Do you hear how fucked up that sounds? Let alone another one of my friends has betrayed my trust."

"I didn't mean it like that, Cherish. What I'm saying is watching you with somebody else helped me realize I was running out of time if I didn't want to lose you for good. For what it's worth, Brittish didn't willingly betray you. I constantly reached out to her to see how you were doing. She blocked me from contacting her a few weeks ago which led to me hiring the investigator."

I wanted to cry, but I didn't have any tears left to shed. I'm emotionally and mentally exhausted. I can't deal with this mess right now, I just can't. "My life had to move forward whether you were around or not. You know what, I'm not doing this with you. I'm not explaining myself or listening to your bullshit after you selfishly chose to follow your dreams. Get out! Get the fuck out, now!"

He kept trying to talk, and I cut him off every time. I didn't care to hear anything he had to say. He should've declared how he felt about us a year ago. He mentioned his number was still the same and informed me how long he'd be in the states before I slammed the door behind him almost snagging his red Polo in the door.

The sweet Cherish was dead and gone. I'm sick and tired of people doing shit to me and thinking an overdue explanation and apology would be enough. I called Brittish to hear the some more fuckery from another so called best friend. If I wasn't talking to Dame since he left, what made her think it was cool to keep the lines of communication open with him? I don't know who's worse, my disloyal best friends or these no good selfish ass niggas.

Brittish picked up the phone happily, I could hear in her voice she was smiling from ear to ear. Too bad I was about to burst that bubble.

"Brittish, you wouldn't believe who showed up at my door after we got off the phone," I spoke in a high-pitched voice sounding fake as hell.

"Who was it, girl? Aaron or Kenly? They need to stop begging for forgiveness and give you some space."

"Nah boo, it was a blast from the past, Dame. Dame from college, the international ball player, showed up at my front door."

Brittish got quiet. "It's funny how you've been helping him keep tabs on me all this time. You sat there and watched me cry knowing he still cared for me. How could you keep talking to him knowing how much our breakup hurt me? You know what, don't say nothing. I'm done with the justifications behind people's terrible actions and behavior."

"It wasn't like that. I know you're tired of hearing everybody's excuses but –"

"But nothing, Britt. I don't have too much to say to you. Enjoy your new house, and take your own advice of giving me some space."

I swallowed the remaining glass of wine and sent my momma a text letting her know I was coming home for Thanksgiving in two weeks. I was planning to be with Aaron this Thanksgiving, but that ship has sail. *"Fuck these trifling ass ungrateful ass selfish ass niggas,"* I said to myself. Ugh, I purposely moved from Charlotte to escape my past, yet my past and present were crashing and burning together.

Chapter 14

Happy Holidays

Cherish

"Ladies and gentlemen, we're about forty-five miles from landing in Memphis. In a moment, you may experience some turbulence. Remember to stay seated if you can." The announcement on the intercom ended.

The flight to Memphis was a little over two hours which was better than a ten-hour drive from Greensboro. The airport was hectic from the holiday traffic as it was the day before Thanksgiving. I grabbed my Jessica Simpson pink luggage set off the conveyor belt heading to the pickup location where my momma should be pulling up at any minute now. Thirty minutes later I put my bags down in my old room, getting settled in, and I spent the remainder of the afternoon having a pajama party with my momma. She had the typical comfort food like ice cream and chocolate Oreos on deck and different wines laid out on the counter. My momma was the realist.

My daddy occasionally stopped in the living room to hear bits and pieces of my drama-filled life. Of course, he suggested I leave these guys alone and wait for the right man to find value in me which I completely agreed with. However, waiting on the one was wearing my patience thin. I waited over a year after Dame left, and I still made a terrible decision when I let Aaron into my life.

Growing tired of the negativity, I let my momma know I didn't want to talk about my problems anymore. The purpose of this visit was to have a pause moment on life and enjoy the holiday with the family, which is exactly what I planned to do for the remainder of the trip.

Thanksgiving Day

The smell of collard greens, ham, and the grease smell from the cornbread made my tummy excited. Lena Wright could cook, and thanks to her, you could tell my ass wasn't missing a meal while I was growing up. I appreciated my natural thickness, but I wasn't trying to go to back to Greensboro with an extra five pounds.

I prepared the dining and living room with enough eating space for twenty or more people and set up a separate table for the kids. Most of my momma's side of the family with a select few people from my daddy's side were coming together for Thanksgiving. I was ready to see my grandmas; I missed my old ladies.

We were expected to eat by two p.m., but in true black people fashion, dinner wasn't ready until four p.m. People spend all day or several days prior preparing the food, yet we still don't eat until damn near Thanksgiving evening. Next year, I'm going to help my momma cook if it means we'll be eating at an earlier time.

One of the younger kids blessed the food, then my nanna banana who is my daddy's mother started passing the food dishes around. I caught up with my cousin Bree and couldn't get enough of pinching my baby cousins' cheeks. It's nothing like family, I'm glad I decided to come home for the holiday.

A couple of hours later, everybody was heading home to get their game plan together to start Black Friday shopping at midnight. I'm a shop alcoholic too, but I'll be pressing an order button online on Cyber

Monday before I'm out and about fighting traffic and dealing with these rude ass people. I continued scrapping the remaining food and residue off the plates as I loaded them into the dishwater. Some Whitney Houston song played from the radio my momma had installed in the kitchen.

"Momma, I love my name, but why did you guys name me Cherish? I know the definition of my name was centered around protection, care, and valuing something, but I feel far from those descriptions. Nobody has taken the time outside of family and my new friend Tori to protect, care, and truly value me."

"Well pumpkin, you're going through a tough moment in life. Many people cherish you, and you know that. You can't let these last few weeks dictate how you view yourself. To be real with you, I had a miscarriage two years before I was blessed to have you. The miscarriage was a hard loss for both your father and I as we desperately wanted to start a family. Your father and I should have come together during that time, but the miscarriage drove a wedge between us. To make a long story short, your father was ready to try again for another baby, but I wasn't ready. Unfortunately, he found comfort in other women from his old job at the Spectrum Center." My jaws dropped. My father was the epitome of what I looked for in a man, but he betrayed my mom in the worst way.

"Don't judge your father for his past mistakes, Cherish. The miscarriage was the first real loss for either of us, and we were young and weren't following God's word yet to handle this loss the right way. He revealed he cheated on me after the mistress had a pregnancy scare. We went to counseling and worked on our marriage. Shortly after, I got pregnant again. We were overjoyed and vowed to value and be devoted to our marriage. It made sense to name you Cherish as your named represented our vows to each other as well as symbolized how grateful we were to be blessed with a daughter." My momma started tearing up like a baby. She's known to get emotional when she talks about motherhood.

"Wow Mommy, that's a lot to take in at once. I would've never thought Daddy would cheat on you. How did you find it in your heart to forgive him?" I reached over to the other side of the counter to turn down the music a bit. I needed make sure I could hear her as I needed some type of advice on how to forgive and move on after the people you love and care about hurt you deeply.

"It wasn't easy, pumpkin. It took several months of counseling, but most of all, I prayed, and God helped me accept nobody's perfect, and we all make mistakes. I know I told you I wasn't going to bring up your situation, but you need to hear this. You must find it in your heart to forgive the people who've done you wrong. It's wearing you down whether you know it or not."

I felt my emotions rising again. Ugh, maybe I needed to seek counseling to get my emotional stability in check. Every time I turned around I was crying over this shit.

"Mommy, it's not easy for me. I'm not you." I cried.

"Cherish, I'm not asking you to be me, all I'm saying is you need to try to forgive. You don't have to remain friends with Brittish or Kenly nor talk to Dame and Aaron again. Sometimes, you forgive people for yourself, not for them. You can't heal if you refuse to forgive."

"I know, Momma, I know. I want to move forward, but it's hard. I wish none of this mess ever happened. What would you do, Momma?" I spoke softly in a cracked-up voice.

"If I were you, I would cut Aaron off, let Dame explain himself, and make amends with your girlfriends. I feel like Aaron plays too many games, and please don't ever disrespect nobody nor yourself by spitting on them, I didn't raise you to be a hood rat. Then, I'm considering how good Dame was to you. Yes, he made mistakes that created a great deal of pain, but like I said, nobody's perfect. Then the situation with your friends wasn't done to intentionally hurt ,you so try to forgive them. They love you and want the best for you. At the end of the day, it's on you what you choose to do with the people in your life."

I continued to clean the kitchen and pondered on everything my momma advised me to do. The ball was in my court, and I was calling all the shots this time around.

Chapter 15

Torn

Cherish

Three Weeks Later...

Another day, another dollar, yet again. I surprised myself this morning by pulling up to work fifteen minutes early. I had Sza's CTRL album blasting through the speakers, as my mind drifted off to the madness that'd occurred over the past month. I came to this city ready for a fresh start and advancing in my career, not for drama, fighting, and endless lies, which is something I've been reminding myself of these last few weeks. It's time for me to move forward not backwards.

Loyalty and trust mean the world to me, and right now, I didn't have either between my friendships and relationships. Whatever with Brittish, and as far as I'm considered, I'm forever good on Aaron and Kenly. I can't dwell on the explanations and excuses; all I could go on was facts, and fact number one is they're dead to me for now. Maybe God will help revive their lives later.

Despite my reservations, I decided to take my momma's advice to hear Dame out. I'm hoping to gain some closure and come to terms with the current state of our relationship once and for all. I reached out to him a few days ago, and he agreed to come by my office during my lunch break. The anxiousness of waiting on twelve-thirty p.m. for this conversation was consuming me. I looked at my Apple watch to check the time realizing this eight-hour workday was scheduled to start in five minutes.

I completed my typical morning routine as usual, enjoying some coffee in my favorite mug that's pink with **boss lady** written in cursive letters. I busied myself with performance reports, but the silence of typing and the clock ticking agitated my nerves. I clicked on Pandora, selecting the Lil' Wayne radio. This radio station would keep me out of my feelings and help me focus on my work as I pretend to sell dope in my mind.

✳✳✳

My office phone lit up taking me out of work mode. "Sorry to bother you, Ms. Wright, but you have a handsome visitor named Dame who's waiting to see you. Should I send him to your office?" Tori asked through the receiver.

"Shoot, my apologies for failing to mention I'd have someone coming through today. I'm headed up front, give me a minute."

I looked in the mirror ensuring that everything was in place, from my hair down to the soles of my feet. I wore a pair of olive colored pants from Fashion Nova that enhanced the size of my booty, paired with a denim shirt and a tan fur vest on top, with dark brown thigh high boots. I took in my appearance once more admiring my new cut and color. Right after turkey day, I went to the salon to switch up my look. I dyed my hair ombre honey blonde and sliced off a few inches into a blunt bob. Somehow cutting my hair made me feel liberated from the past.

I applied a coat of sheer pink lip gloss making my pump lips more enticing. I had no intentions of kissing him or sharing romantic pleasantries, however, it wouldn't hurt to remind him of everything he gave up. The moment I've been anticipating was seconds away from happening.

"Hey Dame, I see you've had the pleasure of meeting my lovely assistant, Tori."

"Oh no, the pleasure was all mine," Tori spoke with a lustful look in her eyes. I felt the desire to get territorial, then I reminded myself Tori wasn't a threat to me. Don't get me wrong, Tori was a baddie, but I am or at least I used to be his treasure, nobody could take my place. Plus, he's not my nigga anymore to be worried about who's checking for him.

"Yeah, Tori made me feel welcomed here and occupied my time while I was waiting on you, gorgeous. Can a nigga get a hug or something?" He ran his hand across my cheek trying to appease me. Back in the day, that gesture would've had me, but the new me wasn't falling for it.

"I would hug you, but my makeup might get on your shirt, and I would hate for the ladies to think you're off the market," I responded back with a sly grin on my face. I knew he was single, but I wouldn't be me if I wasn't shady. Then he got the nerve to show up at my office looking all daddyish. His hair was freshly done in two French braids while he's wearing a black Givenchy sweater, black jeans, and red leather Giuseppe Zanotti. Goddamn, it should be illegal to be that fine. There was no way I could hug him without wanting to do more.

"Aite, I see how it is. You know I've never cared if you wore makeup, and I've never been the type to deal with groupies. You're acting like you don't know me no more."

"Tuhh, I'm not acting, Dame. It's been a year and half since I've seen you, so miss me with the nothing has changed bullshit," I stated, smacking my lips. Dame's eyebrows furrowed together confirming he was shocked to hear me carrying on like this. I was no longer the good girl that carried her emotions on their sleeve, these past few weeks have turned me into a savage. Well...maybe not a savage, but I'm tired of people talking to me crazy and thinking I'm supposed to take their shit. Nah, not anymore!

To avoid the conversation going awry, I headed towards the elevator, hoping he'd get the cue to follow me. "I'll be back in an hour, Tori. You know the drill, forward calls and take down important messages. Thank you for all that you do!"

I stepped on the elevator with him right at my heels, pressing the clear button for the ground floor. The ride down was quiet; however, the silence couldn't last much longer. The purpose of him coming to my job was for us to talk not for me to get in a mood and start acting like a bitch. Lately, my emotions have been all over the place, and his little comment shouldn't have bothered me that bad. I thought about apologizing to him, but I was in an unapologetic mood for the moment. The bell rang, elevator doors opened, and we headed for the glass double doors leading to the sidewalk.

"Looks like it's me and you for the next hour, where do you want to go?" Dame asked.

"I want to go to LeBauer Park. It's food truck Friday downtown, and I'm starving," I replied, making sure to walk a few steps ahead of him. He picked up his pace to keep up with me.

"My bad for coming at you like that. No, I haven't physically been a part of your life in quite some time but following up on you made me feel like I still knew you. I'm going to always care about how you're doing, Cherish."

I gave him a nonchalant shoulder shrug letting him know I was listening. I could feel his pretty green eyes staring at me, admiring my natural beauty as a light breeze filled the atmosphere. I knew Dame wanted us to remain friends, but back then, I wasn't strong enough to just be his friend. The saying "You can never just be friends with somebody you love" was too true for me. Although Brittish was dead wrong for keeping this a secret, it's heartwarming to know he still cared enough about me to constantly make sure I was good.

"Can I get the two-piece fried tilapia with seasoned fries and a large Sprite?" I asked the guy behind the window of the Fish N Chip's food truck. I fixed my lips to ask Dame if he wanted some food, but he shook his head no.

"It's eight-dollars-and-twenty-five-cents, ma'am." I reached into my back pocket for some cash when Dame handed the man a twenty-dollar bill and let him know he could keep the change. Ain't shit changed about him. He's still the caring person I fell in love with almost three years ago.

I took my food from the cashier wondering how I was going to walk, eat, and manage not to spill my drink. A few seconds passed by before I asked for some help.

"Do you mind holding my drink…. please?" I said sweetly, batting my curled eyelashes. I'm a trip going from being a pain in the ass to acting nice the moment I need him to do something for me.

"I was waiting on you to ask," he responded, letting out a playful laugh that created a sparkle in his eyes.

I sensed my heart racing and butterflies in my stomach, he still had a hold on me.

"Let's stop here," I suggested once I spotted a brick bench near the fountain. The sunny weather mixed with the sweet melodies from the live jazz band was lightening up my mood. I finished wiping my hands and mouth with a napkin preparing myself for this dreaded talk.

"Why have you been so pressed to see me? I know I'm still fine like wine, but I thought those Italian women had you wrapped around their fingers."

He stared at me hard. "The only woman that's had me wrapped around her finger was you. I miss you, Cherish. I miss you so much, baby. My biggest regret was leaving you. I never wanted to hurt you." He sounded so genuine and sincere. "You don't know how hard it was to see you smiling and posted up with somebody else on social media." His nose flared up for a second signifying his anger.

I sat my food to the side, instantly losing my appetite. I took a few deep breaths attempting to calm my heart and mind down. A part of me felt like jumping over the moon because I always wondered if he still cared, whereas the other part of me wanted to say fuck him.

"Honestly, I miss you too, Dame, but you can't sit here and tell me you didn't mean to hurt me. I was heartbroken when we dropped you off at the airport. I cried in your momma's arms and kept crying for weeks! I know Brittish told you how much I was hurting. You waited all this time to put an end to my broken heart." I repeatedly blinked back a few tears before one fell, staining my right cheek.

He turned his body towards me, putting his calloused hand over mine. "I'm sorry, Cherish. I swear to God I'm so sorry for hurting you. It was an unexpected decision between you or my career, and back then, I didn't think it was possible to have both. I was a newbie to the game, and I was going to be thousands of miles away. Let's be real, maintaining a relationship would've been unrealistic. Before I let this industry damage you or the memories we shared, I knew it was best to end things, or at least I thought that was the best thing to do at the time."

I remained speechless with a resting bitch face refusing to show any type of emotion. He was right, but I didn't plan on letting him know that. Everybody knows a baller lifestyle can get chaotic from practices, games, and the groupies. Dame's a good man, but even good guys fall victim to this demanding lifestyle. However, I knew he would get drafted eventually, and I was prepared to ride with him till the very end even if it meant being a twelve-hour plane ride away.

He got down on his knees in between my legs, holding onto my waist as he proceeded to say, "Cherish Renee Wright, I love you more than you'll ever know, and I'll do whatever it takes to show you that I need you in my life. What's the point of the cars, money, and my career if it doesn't involve you? I'll pay for you to fly back and forth to see me until I secure a contract to play for a team on the east coast. Matter fact come spend Christmas with me in Italy. I know this is a lot all at once, but promise me you'll think about it?" He gave me the puppy dog eyes trying to manipulate my feelings.

"Move, get up!" He gave me the 'you can't be serious right now' look, and the mean mug I sported with my left eyebrow arched let him know I was serious as hell.

"You can't just show up at my job, confess your feelings, and think I'm going to be down for your little plan. Yes, I love you, Dame, and I've dreamed for way too long of the day we'd reconnect, but I'm not the woman I used to be."

I planted my feet on the concrete making sure to fix my shirt when I stood up. "If you couldn't tell, I love hard to the point where I give too much and start to lose myself. After everything that's happened to me recently, I've come to realize men, including you, only care about themselves. Do you hear yourself right now? Everything you're saying is all about you. From your suggestion that I would be the only one doing the traveling back and forth to your decision of us parting ways solely based on your career. Not once did you ask me how I felt!"

At this point, I was doing the ugly cry with black tears falling down my cheeks from the mascara. Spectators were starting to stop and stare at us. "Cherish, stop crying. I'm sorry, I didn't mean to disregard your feelings. I can admit my decision and current proposition was selfish. Let me rephrase some things."

He was still on his knees looking ridiculous when he reached out to rest his arms around my thick thighs. "I'm proud of the life you've created for yourself, and I pray you consider letting me be a part of it. I know how bad I hurt you, and I meant it when I said I'm willing to do whatever to get you back. The ball is in your court, sweetheart. Just know I love you, and our love was and could still be the realest."

I wanted to scream at the top of my lungs, but I settled for saying, "GRRRR!" My emotions were switching back and forth between being angry, sad, and happy. I was mad as a firecracker because he waited so long before he attempted to make things right. Then sadness took over because I love him, but happiness set in because he still loves me too. I wanted to cave in and say yes, but my trust and emotional stability were all kinds of fucked up and dealing with a man was my last priority. I'm a hopeless romantic, but this time around, I'm taking care of me, and there's not enough room to care of him right now.

"Our love was the realest, it truly was, but I can't do this. If you love me as much as you proclaim you do, you'll let me be." I pried his hands off me, anticipating the moment of getting off work early and drowning my sorrows with a bottle of wine.

I managed to walk a few feet away before I broke down on the sidewalk. My head was pounding from racing thoughts and crying uncontrollably. I felt myself struggling to breathe when I heard the faint sound of his voice saying, "Wait. Noooo! Cherish, you didn't mean ---" before everything went black.

I blinked my eyes open being blinded by bright white lights on the ceiling. I heard a beeping noise, turning my head slightly to the left to see a hospital monitor. When I turned around to my right, Dame stood by my bedside.

"You're awake, beautiful. Let me call the nurse." The appearance of his face helped me recall the intense conversation we were having, but everything after that was a blur.

"What happened, Dame? The last thing I remember is walking away from you."

He grabbed my hand. "Yeah, you walked away, and I called out to you trying to convince you not to leave me, then the next thing I know, I was watching you fall out on the cement. I told the doctor I was your boyfriend, but due to patient rights, the nurse only told me you were dehydrated."

If only I had the energy to cuss him out for lying to the doctor. There was a light tap-tap sound against the door, then the nurse strolled in.

"Hello, Ms. Wright, it's nice to see you're awake. I'm Nurse Pratt. How are you feeling?" she stated before she started checking my vitals and documenting it on my chart.

I sat up in the bed. "I'm feeling better. What happened? Why do I have an IV in my arm?" A plethora of questions were dancing around in my mind.

"I'm going to answer your questions, but I would like for Mr. Westbrook to step out unless you want him to stay."

"Thanks for being here, Dame, but can you wait outside?" He shook his head yes in agreement.

"Have you ever had a problem with anxiety?" I gave her a confused look, shaking my head yes. I've heard of anxiety, and I've joked around being an emotional wreck, but shoot, everybody gets anxious and emotional sometimes, no biggie.

"The reason I asked you this is because you had an acute anxiety attack combined with dehydration. Mr. Westbrook disclosed the nature of the conversation and presenting symptoms prior to seeing you pass out. Symptoms of anxiety could be sweating, stress, shortness of breath, etcetera. Do you recall any of those symptoms before you passed out?"

"Yeah... I remember feeling extremely upset, and I felt like I couldn't breathe."

"It's normal to experience anxiety, however, your anxiety became too much for your body which is one of the reasons you passed out. Sometimes, your body shuts down when you're anxious or other emotions become uncontrollable. Here's a brochure about anxiety for future reference." I did an overview of the pamphlet before I tossed it to the side, I'd read it later.

"Didn't you mention dehydrated? I'm a bit confused; it's winter time, people don't get dehydrated."

"Ms. Wright, you're partially correct. Dehydration is more profound during the summertime, but there are other non-weather reasons related to dehydration. The IV is running fluids to hydrate your body. I'm advising you to rest this weekend and make it a priority to drink water, sports drinks, or something to keep you hydrated.

"Okay, I can handle that. When will I be discharged?"

"In a few hours the discharge nurse will bring in your discharge papers, but I want to monitor you a little while longer." She flipped through some more papers in my chart while I grabbed my phone off the tray near the bed. I started to call Brit and Ken, but I remembered we're at war right now. I locked my phone figuring I could take an Uber to retrieve my car then I could head home. I couldn't take dealing with Dame again if the first go around led to an anxiety attack. I'm telling you, men only create problems.

"Ms. Wright, I'm not sure if you're aware of this, but your blood test shows you're pregnant. Being pregnant is another explanation for being dehydrated." My eyes got big as saucers. Ain't no way, ain't no fucking way I'm pregnant.

"Pregnant...hmm, are you sure, Ms, Pratt?" My brows furrowed together praying she read my chart wrong.

"Yes, I'm sure, Ms. Wright. You're certainly pregnant, congratulations! I'm sure whatever you and your boyfriend were arguing about will be old news once he finds about the baby. We can do an ultrasound before you leave to confirm how many weeks you are." I let her know I'd do the ultrasound, but I didn't want Dame to know yet.

"The nurse will be back to check on you in an hour. It's pertinent to remain stress free and take better care of your health. You have a little one to be considerate of now." She smiled on her exit out as if having a baby was the greatest blessing. I've dreamed of having kids, but not right now, not like this.

I closed my eyes attempting to process everything that's happened in one day from Dame begging me to take him back to learning I'm having Aaron's baby.

Why lord, why? was my current thought. For the second time in my life hearing the words "You're pregnant" couldn't have come at a worse time.

Dame reentered the room with a look of concern. "What did the doctor say? Are you going to be okay?" I contemplated on how much of the truth to share with him.

"Yes, I'm fine. She explained I was dehydrated, and I'll be discharged in a few hours. Do you mind going to Tropical Smoothie, I want a Kiwi Quencher?"

He kissed my forehead, agreeing to whatever I asked for, and let me know to call if I wanted anything else.

"I'm so glad you're going to be alright, don't ever scare me like that again. And by the way, I've decided to opt out of my contract during the mid-season trade. In roughly two months, I'll be back in the states for good, and I'm going to see what my playing options are on the east coast. They say anything worth having is worth fighting for, and you're worth the fight. I love you too much to let you go again." He blew me a kiss before the door closed behind him.

A few tears fell from my eyes. I often prayed for the day God would bless me with another baby, but it wasn't supposed to be like this.

TO BE CONTINUED...

To my readers: Thank you for giving me a chance as a new author. It feels like a dream come to true to self-publish my first book. Please leave reviews, I want to hear your feedback. Stay tuned for part 2, coming soon.

ABOUT THE AUTHOR

Erica Nicole was born on August 23rd in a small town called Snow Hill, NC and moved to Greensboro, NC to attend The University of NC at Greensboro where she graduated in May 2016 with a B.A in psychology and minor in English. She's always been an avid reader and at the young age of eight she knew she wanted to write books one day. Her love for reading started with children books, then African American literature such as November Blues by Sharon Draper, and transitioned to Erotic and Urban Fiction after reading Zane and Jade Jones books. She knew she was going to take writing serious after her high school English teacher, K. Williams told some of my classmates including herself that they should get their short stories published. 8 years later she started her publishing company Best Publications and penned her first novel, The Ultimate Betrayal: A 336

Love Story which debuted October 2018. As a new indie author she looks forward to penning many more novels pertaining to Urban Roman and African American literature.

Stay Connected with Best Publications
IG: enbestpublications
Facebook Like Page: Best Publications Presents
Reading Group: Literacy Sweethearts
Website: www.enbestpublications.com
Email: enbestpublications@gmail.com

www.ingramcontent.com/pod-product-compliance
Lightning Source LLC
Chambersburg PA
CBHW032007240626
47153CB00003B/1153